Mi...

NATALIE FOX

Heartline
Books

Published by Heartline Books Limited in 2002

Copyright © Natalie Fox 2002

Natalie Fox has asserted her rights under the Copyright, Designs and Patents Act, 1988 to be identified as the author of this work.

This is a work of fiction. Names and characters are the product of the author's imagination and any resemblance to any actual persons, living or dead, is purely coincidental.

All rights reserved. No part of this publication may be reproduced, stored in or introduced into a retrieval system or transmitted by any form, or by any means (electronic, mechanical, photocopying, recording or otherwise) without the prior written permission of the publisher. Any person who takes any unauthorised action in relation to this publication may be liable to criminal prosecution and civil claims for damages.

Heartline Books Limited and Heartline Books logo are trademarks of the publisher.

First published in the United Kingdom in 2002 by Heartline Books Limited.

Heartline Books Limited
PO Box 22598, London W8 7GB

Heartline Books Ltd. Reg No: 03986653

ISBN 1-903867-36-3

Styled by Oxford Designers & Illustrators

Printed and bound in Great Britain by
Cox & Wyman, Reading, Berkshire

NATALIE FOX

NATALIE FOX was born and educated in London and had a variety of jobs before she decided to become a writer. 'I can't believe I once delivered sandwiches around Soho, on a scooter!' Natalie says 'I chose to write romantic fiction because I am the heroine of *all* my novels and that means I can get to *grips* with the most gorgeous men in the world!'

While living in Spain, Natalie and her husband adopted two little cats who were down on their luck. They brought them back to Wales, where the couple now live in a tiny village, with a river running through the garden. It's the most perfect place in the world because of the beautiful scenery – and it's even next door to the pub!

The author's claims 'My passions in life are my husband, my work, cats, gardens, hot, hot curries, jazz and EastEnders. I love trips to London where I shop till my husband drops and I love holidays in hot places. One of the things I hate is…custard tarts!'

The response to Natalie Fox's first Heartline novel, LOVE IS FOREVER, has been overwhelming. One reviewer said 'I can't think of a better book to launch Heartline than this book. I was impressed by the quality if Natalie Fox's writing and am looking forward to reading many more Heartline romances by this talented author.'

YESTERDAY'S MAN, Natalie's second Heartline novel, proved very popular with readers. If you missed it, and would like to read it, why not write to us at P O Box 22598, London W8 7GB, enclosing a cheque or postal order for £4.49 (inc. p&p) and we'll send you the book by return.

Heartline Books – Romance at its best

Call the Heartline Hotline on 0845 6000 504 and order any book you may have missed – you can now pay over the phone by credit or debit card.

Have you visited the Heartline website yet?

If you haven't – and even for those of you who have – it's well worth a trip as we are constantly updating our site.

So log on to www.heartlinebooks.com where you can...

- ♥ Order one or more books – including titles you may have missed – and pay by credit or debit card
- ♥ Check out special offers and events, such as celebrity interviews
- ♥ Find details of our writing classes for aspiring authors
- ♥ Read more about Heartline authors
- ♥ Enter competitions
- ♥ Browse through our catalogue

And much, much more...

chapter one

'*Jenna can marry whoever she likes! After all this time do you think I care what she* does with her frivolous life?'

Ross Cameron stood by the window of the Cameron Holdings boardroom, gazing down at the River Thames below, his own words bitten out indignantly to his father earlier, still ringing in his ears. The murky waters swirling in the mist of a grey London day seemed to punch at the dark side of his conscience. The dark side where Jenna still troubled him after all these years.

The shuffle of his senior directors leaving the room behind him made no inroads into the dark thoughts which had disturbed him throughout the meeting. The silence after their subdued exit did at last though.

This was ridiculous. Why should he let that wild child encroach into his successful life yet again? She was history and he had meant what he had said to his father before the meeting; he didn't care who she married. As for his father's request, that he go to Paris to stop her wedding...Alastair Cameron must have suffered a brainstorm!

With ice cool determination Ross forced himself to concentrate on the order of the day and what had transpired at the recent board meeting: the take-over.

He turned to his father who had founded the company and knew what was coming as he watched him rise wearily from the table and make for the courtesy bar to pour two drinks. There would be the usual lecture on his son's ruthlessness, how different it was from his days as Chairman of the board. Though Ross had done nothing illegal he had rather gone for the jugular on this one, and against a personal friend of his father's. He had further cause to be troubled with his conscience today.

His father came and stood by his side at the window, as tall and broad as his only son and handed him a crystal tumbler of whisky.

'I suppose you are expecting a slap on the back and congratulations?' Alastair began and before he could add anymore Ross held his free hand up to still him. Neither looked at each other. Both stared bleakly out of the window with the same cool gaze.

'I've heard it all before, father,' he said tightly. 'I did what had to be done. I know you and Edward go back a long way but times have changed. Edward can retire gracefully now and spend the rest of his days on the golf course.'

'With his damned spirit broken,' Alastair growled. 'You're a hard one these days, Ross.'

'I've been well tutored by you,' Ross muttered under his breath.

Alastair shook his head. 'I don't think I've ever plummeted such depths of ruthlessness. Brookmans was Edward's life and you've just snatched it from him, coldly, clinically and —'

'And I've done him a favour,' Ross retorted sharply and turned to his father, his handsome features grave and set. 'And one day he'll thank me for it and perhaps one day you will give me the full credit for what you have made me into. The mirror image of yourself!' His fist tightened around the tumbler. 'Twenty years ago you would have done the very same thing,' he condescended in a controlled tone. 'You're going soft in your old age, father. And we both know who is responsible. Jenna's mother, Yvonne; your third wife, remember?' he grated sarcastically and turned away from his father to refill his glass.

Remorse struck Ross as the amber liquid hit the bottom of the tumbler. He shouldn't have sounded so scathing. He'd only brought it up because of the mention of Jenna before this meeting. It had put his whole being on edge. An apology wouldn't come easily to his lips though for that grim reminder of something that was still an ache in his father's heart. It was one of those unwelcome character genes he had inherited; a streak of stubbornness like the one that had caused the rift between his father and his now estranged wife, French born Yvonne. She had returned to Paris after the split and lived there with her errant daughter, Jenna.

In a way, Ross could sympathise with his father's failings where Yvonne was concerned. Like himself Alastair found it almost impossible to back down, admit to a mistake and actually apologise for it. Pride should be the Camerons' middle name, he thought ruefully. Both Cameron men were stuffed with it.

Yvonne had been Alastair's failure, and Jenna? Was she forever to be a thorn in Ross's side? An inward shudder chilled down his spine and he swallowed a mouthful of Scotch to quell it.

From that first moment Yvonne had brought her into

their lives, her only daughter from one of her previous marriages, she had rattled Ross's cage. At the time she had been a pretty raven haired fifteen-year-old with astonishing smoky grey eyes; thin as a bone, fragile but with the mind and attitude of a thirty-year-old vamp. She was wild, arrogant, precocious, spoilt beyond measure, his worst teenage nightmare.

As a twenty-four-year-old, he was just back from the States with an armful of business degrees and ready to rise swiftly in his father's corporation. In America, he had thought he had seen it all, but Jenna? Never in his life had he met anyone like her. She wore skirts up to her armpits, plastered her face with ghoulish make up, streaked her long raven hair with slashes of purple and, coupled with her bad taste appearance, she had a mouth that spat fire. Mostly in Ross's direction. It was all they had in common, their utter contempt for each other.

'Yvonne needs our help with this one, Ross. She doesn't want Jenna marrying this Marcel DeLuc,' Ross heard his father mutter behind him as he paced the room now.

Ross spun round to face him. 'And I told you before the meeting that this has nothing to do with us!' he told him.

'God damn it, Ross,' Alastair exploded. 'Jenna is part of the family and –'

'No way!' Ross laughed thinly. 'Jenna is the daughter of one of Yvonne's ex-husbands. She's nothing to do with us. She's trouble; always has been and always will be. She's Yvonne's responsibility, not yours or mine.'

'And if Yvonne and I were still together she would

be my responsibility,' Alastair insisted, glaring at his son darkly.

Ross clenched his fists in an effort to cool himself down. 'But you're not still together,' he reasoned wearily. 'Yvonne walked out on you three years ago because of lack of attention on your part. You always did put business before everything in your life,' he told him, not regretting having to point out his father's failure. Sometimes the truth was best laid out on the mortuary slab of good intentions.

'I know you are still suffering regrets over the split,' he went on more calmly, 'and admittedly you are still keeping in touch, but it's unfair of Yvonne to ask this of you. Jenna is a wild card and if she wants to marry she's old enough now to please herself.'

There was a long pause before his father let out a long sigh. 'As you well know, Ross, Jenna has never had a very firm grasp on reality.'

Ross's eyes went skywards at the absurd realism of that statement. Jenna lived on a different astral plane from the rest of mortals. It was difficult to accept that she hadn't been created on the planet Mars and deposited on Earth to cause mayhem for the whole world!

'Well it seems she has now,' Ross reasoned. 'She's going to be married and these days that's a pretty real thing to be contemplating.' He went to his father and took the empty tumbler from his hand. 'Another?'

Alastair nodded, slumped heavily into his leather boardroom chair and raked a hand through his still-thick mass of silver hair.

Ross studied him worriedly after he had poured him

another drink and handed it to him. He tugged at the trouser leg of his immaculate navy blue suit and perched on the edge of the long mahogany table. He thought his father had been coping with Yvonne's defection rather well but now Alistair's unhappiness was showing in the gravity of his features again, and all because of Jenna. Always Jenna. If Ross had been a gambling man he would have put money on the fact that three years previously Jenna had encouraged her mother to leave his father. She always had tried to cause trouble between them. Snappy little remarks about Alastair not being her real father so why should she be forced to live by his rules. Ross used to feel the full force of her fury too, when he was around, though he had tried to *avoid* being around when Jenna was at home because she was so obnoxiously irritating.

'Let this one go, father,' Ross earnestly pleaded with him. 'You've always done your best for Jenna but unfortunately it was never appreciated. Yvonne has always spoilt her. But it's all in the past now. After all this time Yvonne has no right to ask for your help to stop her daughter's marriage.'

'We are still man and wife. Neither of us has done anything about a divorce. She has no one else to turn to,' Alistair said flatly.

'Maybe so,' Ross returned with a resigned sigh, 'but she left you, after all. As for me going to Paris to sort this out for you...' he shook his head firmly. 'No, father. One look at me and Jenna will be even more determined to go through with the wedding.' Ross got up from the table and started to gather up sheaves of papers after the meeting. 'There's no love lost between us, father. Three years without a sight of each other won't have changed a thing.'

'I always thought you and Jenna might have –'

Ross laughed cynically, cutting him off in mid sentence. 'Ah, "the best laid plans of mice and men",' he quoted sarcastically; remembering how, at every opportunity, his father and Yvonne had tried to throw them together. 'Never in a million years. Jenna and I are poison together. Always have been, always will be.' The words came out in a leaden tone but Alistair was so deep in thought that Ross knew he wouldn't notice.

The very mention of Jenna was enough to get that damned conscience of his rattling its chains again. Once, just once he had done something deeply regretful where Jenna was concerned. A moment of sheer madness that had had dreadful repercussions on his life. A moral aberration that he knew he would have to live with for ever. Time wasn't a great healer as some pundit had once stated. Ross knew that the guilt got ever worse with each passing day. Now it was at full throttle and all because of news of this impending wedding which should have gone some way towards easing his guilt. Jenna happily married to someone else would surely soothe his troubled conscience where she was concerned.

Ross straightened his tall frame and felt an odd pull at his heart. He rubbed his chest, wondered at the feeling, and decided that he did have a heart after all. He knew Jenna's history, that she had never known her real father, then Yvonne had had a second troubled marriage, before she'd married Alistair. That second marriage had ended in a bitter divorce which must have affected Jenna. Ross understood her troubled background, and thought that though she had been cushioned by wealth, it still sounded like some tragic melodrama. She'd been pushed from one boarding school to another, scarcely having time to settle and make friends. But it was difficult to sympathise with someone as wildly arrogant and uncontrollable as she had been. Compared to some poor children in the world her troubles had been minor.

But once he had shown her affection and sympathy and where had it led? He shivered again and turned his attention away from his father to pack his briefcase.

'I'm pleading with you to go to Paris, Ross,' Alastair said gravely. 'We can't stand back and let her make this mistake. This Marcel DeLuc isn't right for her. You must have read about him.'

'Yes, I have. Who hasn't?' Ross stated wryly. 'Last year he was engaged to be married to a Danish actress..., the year before –'

'Exactly why he isn't a suitable husband for Jenna. The damned man has a track record of affairs as long as my arm! He's nothing more than a playboy. His father might be a politician but –'

'Marcel DeLuc is a very successful modern artist in his own right,' Ross interjected. 'OK, he courts publicity across Europe, some of it sensational, and now he's going to marry Jenna.' Ross smiled ruefully. 'I'd say it was a marriage made in heaven.'

'Where's your damned heart, Ross?' Alastair reasoned forcefully.

'In my boots where it always has been where Jenna is concerned,' Ross told him cryptically. 'You have a short memory, father. I haven't. I remember every last insult that girl rang into your ears and mine. I remember the tantrums, the constant aggro when she was in the house.'

'She was just a kid, a troubled one at that. You always did take her too seriously.' Alastair suddenly grinned. 'She was a helluva fireball at fifteen,' he mused fondly.

'And at sixteen, and seventeen and now at twenty-four she is probably still firing on all cylinders,' Ross retorted flintily, snapping shut his briefcase.

Alastair shrugged. 'Yvonne did say Jenna had mellowed a little in these past years.'

'Even a great chunk of mellow on Jenna's part would still win her the trouble of the year prize,' Ross said tightly. 'Now forget all this, Father. I don't want to hear any more about it. Right, I'm off. I've a meeting with Patersons this afternoon, I'm dining with Karen tonight and I'll be back at my apartment around midnight if you need me.'

'Still seeing Karen Martin, are you? It's about time you married the girl and put her out of her misery,' Alastair said as he got to his feet.

Ross smiled, glad his father had got off the uncomfortable subject of Jenna's forthcoming wedding. 'It's not that sort of a relationship,' he informed him tightly. 'Neither of us wants a firm commitment. From what I've seen of marriage, I'll give it a miss thanks.'

'If that's a direct dig at my track record, save your sarcasm for your business meetings, Ross,' Alastair returned sharply. 'If your mother was still alive you'd have a less cynical attitude towards marriage and my failings at it.' He sighed deeply and reflectively. 'She was my life till she lost hers,' he said softly. Then he shrugged. 'My marriage to Felicity was a weak attempt to get over her. The divorce was mercifully painless for us both. We are all allowed one mistake,' he said sagely as father and son moved out of the boardroom to the lifts.

'How about two? Yvonne was another mistake,' Ross commented as he punched the lift button. Though at the time he hadn't thought that way. He'd liked Yvonne immensely and had hoped that she was indeed the one to bring his father happiness; herself come to that, but it hadn't worked out.

'I truly loved Yvonne,' Alastair said with uncharacteristic wistfulness. 'I still do love her, but,' he shrugged yet again, 'some things are just meant to be. Like you I can pull off a deal at the drop of the hat, but emotions...' he shook his head as they stepped into the chrome lift. 'Tricky business, love.'

'I wouldn't know,' Ross muttered as he stabbed at the ground floor button.

He'd managed to steer well clear of affairs of the heart. It was why Karen suited him so well; she made no emotional demands that he was incapable of meeting. A dedicated career woman herself, she was indeed the perfect companion.

Companion, he mused, as the lift whooshed them down eight floors. The description sounded archaic to say the least. But then Jenna had always accused him of being cold – a stuffed shirt, with less emotion than a mushroom; descriptions of his character that had on occasion brought a rare smile to his face. *Get a life*, was one of her stock phrases, always thrown at him with a vengeance, always without comment from him. That was what had rattled her most, the fact she couldn't arouse his temper, until she had once, just once. It was something he was so deeply regretful over that he knew it would be with him for life, a mental scar to bear for ever.

'Have you got a chill coming on?' Alastair asked as they stepped out into the columned marble foyer of the Cameron Holdings building.

'A chill?'

'You shivered just then.'

Ross felt as if Jenna was walking over his grave but he didn't tell Alistair. His father thought him ruthless enough already, so to admit to what had once happened between him and Jenna would confirm him as the "devil's sidekick". In spite of the battles between them which they both considered normal in a business relationship as well as that of father and son, Ross didn't want to lose his father's respect, which he knew was unwavering. And his father would be horrified if he knew what had been troubling Ross all these years.

'The wind-down after the meeting,' Ross told him, in explanation for that cold shiver from the past, as they strode through the foyer to their waiting chauffeur-driven cars. 'And perhaps a thread of regret that you think I pulled a fast one on Edward by whipping his corporation out from under him.'

His father turned to him before they parted company and smiled thinly. He took Ross's hand and shook it formally.

'It was a good deal, son,' he told him seriously. 'I'm proud of you. Forgive me for snapping at you but I've a soft spot for Edward. I might have handled things differently, but the outcome would have been the same, I guess. Forget anything I said. You're right, I must be going soft.' He sighed heavily. 'Now all this business with Jenna.' He shook his head again. 'Yvonne sounded distraught on the phone. She doesn't know which way to turn on this one. At first she tried to talk Jenna out of it but came up against a brick wall.'

'Bad mistake on Yvonne's part then,' Ross commented, wishing his father hadn't brought the subject up again. 'The only way to get Jenna to co-operate is to advise the opposite of what you want her to do. If Yvonne was over the moon about the wedding Jenna wouldn't be so determined to go through with it. But let's be charitable about all this and tell ourselves that Jenna is really happy, head over heels in love with the man.'

'How can she be? He might be a successful artist but he still has the reputation of being a womaniser and rebel.'

Ross grimaced. 'Do I have to say it yet again, Father? They are admirably suited to each other. They can both rebel away to their heart's content.'

Ross saw the pain in his father's eyes at that cryptic remark and softened his approach slightly after glancing at his watch. He didn't want to be late for the Patersons meeting.

'Go to Paris if you must, father,' he suggested.' If you feel so strongly about it all, go and put your point of view. But I tell you, you will be wasting your time. Jenna will do her own thing just as she has all her life.'

'The request was for you to go, Ross, not me,' Alastair reminded him in subdued tones. 'When I told you about it before the meeting I led you to believe that I wanted you to go in my place. But that isn't the case. Yvonne wants you over there, not me. She specifically asked for you to go. Make of that what you will.'

A sharp wind suddenly burst into the pillared entrance enclosure outside the building. Ross smoothed back his dark hair as if guilt were responsible for the sudden gust. Why should Yvonne want him to go? Had Jenna confided in her mother, told her what had happened between them so long ago?

Still no reason for Yvonne to summon him to Paris to stop her daughter's wedding. More than likely she couldn't face Alastair, and Ross was next on the helpline, though she knew well enough the animosity which existed between her only daughter and her estranged husband's only son. It was a strange request and puzzled him but he didn't question his father any further.

'I'll give it some thought, father,' he told him just to end the subject for the time being. 'I'll call you later.'

The chauffeurs were patiently waiting to open the doors of the limousines for them and Ross escorted his father to his car. 'Where are you going?' he asked as Alastair slid into the back of the car.

'The club of course. It's where redundant chairmen of the board go to drown their sorrows and reminisce over great past transactions. Edward will be there of course and I'll have to tell him the bad news; he doesn't have a company anymore. You own it, lock, stock and barrel.'

'*We* own it, father. We *are* still partners and it's *good* news for Edward,' Ross corrected. 'And remind him that we've greased his palm with ten million so that should ease the grief.'

Alastair smiled ruefully. 'It'll buy a helluva lot of malt whisky.'

'That's the spirit,' Ross laughed and his father frowned at the rather weak joke and lifted a hand to signal his driver on.

Ross sank into the leather plushness of his own Rolls Royce and closed his eyes for a few seconds. He wasn't usually so weary after a meeting. The rush of adrenaline usually carried him over a few days.

It was Jenna of course, he realised. Twenty-two miles of Channel and a few motorways between them and she could still get to him. He felt the tension in his chest. Damn her! Why couldn't she have eloped with the Frenchman and put them all out of their misery? She was probably enjoying all the furore surrounding her choice of husband. It was probably the main objective; to have everyone rushing around her in state of turmoil while she was laughing at them all behind their backs. Because love had nothing to do with all this. Jenna was incapable of love. She was just attention-seeking as usual.

'Where to, Sir?' Anthony requested and as Ross opened his eyes he realised his chauffeur's query was a repeat.

'Um, Patersons, Docklands,' he uttered absently. He glanced at his watch and then pressed his fists against his brow. 'Take the long route, Anthony. Take any of the bridges and drive along the Embankment. Slowly.'

'Time to kill, Sir?' Anthony smiled as he pulled away from the kerb.

'In a manner of speaking,' Ross mumbled and closed his eyes again. He'd give anything to kill that memory, of Jenna's eighteenth birthday. He wished he could remove it permanently from his mind but that had always been impossible.

Jenna's eighteenth birthday...

chapter two

His father had telephoned him at his Knightsbridge apartment from Paris. Ross had just got home and was about to shower before going out for the night. With which female he couldn't now recall. Early evening drinks before a concert followed by supper at Pierre's, was his usual programme.

'Ross, we've been held up I'm afraid,' his father had said regretfully. 'Yvonne is distraught that we won't make it back to celebrate Jenna's birthday. Do the honours, son. Drive down to Sussex and take her out to dinner tonight. Yvonne called her earlier and explained we can't make it and you'll be down. Poor kid's on her own, rattling around the Hall, wondering what to do with herself.'

Ross had looked at his watch and closed his eyes in disbelief. Jenna rattling around wondering what to do with herself on her birthday was hardly likely in anyone's wildest dreams. At this very minute she was probably struggling into a sexy skimpy outfit that defied credibility and heading for some ghastly London nightspot from where she would emerge at dawn, flushed, dishevelled and slightly dizzy, and yet prepared to start all over again.

'I've got a date, father, and I'm the last person Jenna would want to deliver birthday wishes.' Ross had offered impatiently. 'I'm sure she'll be all right.'

'For goodness sake, Ross, have a heart. Yvonne said Jenna was really disappointed we couldn't make it. It's her birthday after all.'

It had been on the tip of Ross's tongue to point out that he and Yvonne should have thought of that sooner but he'd held back. If his father had been delayed it was probably something to do with business and for a fraction of a moment his sympathies went out to Yvonne and Jenna.

'OK, I'll go down and smooth her feathers,' he offered in resignation. 'Don't worry, I'll make it up to her.'

He had regretfully cancelled his date, angry with his father for disrupting his evening and then almost immediately angry with himself for having forgotten Jenna's birthday anyway.

He'd salved his conscience by carefully selecting a rather beautiful perfect single pearl on a gold chain for her, just catching the jewellers before closing time.

En route to Sussex he gathered up more gifts, flowers and chocolates from the motorway services, telling himself that he was probably wasting his time and money because, knowing Jenna, she wouldn't be in when he got there anyway.

And who could blame her he finally asked himself. The prospect of spending such a special birthday with him for sole company was as bad for her as it was for him. What the hell would they talk about over dinner? They had absolutely nothing in common.

As soon as he pulled into the long drive of Amersham Hall, deep in the heart of rural Sussex, he knew he had underestimated her yet again. The drive and the huge circular frontage to the mansion were heaving with cars and battered vans. One drawn up at the foot of the stone steps had a mobile disco company logo emblazoned on its side, complete with flames licking the side of the old rust bucket. Another van advertised the culinary skills of a well known catering group.

He could't help thinking what a waste Jenna was to humanity. With her verve and vitality she could have been employed stopping wars. In only a matter of hours she had organised a party, complete with disco and catering and goodness knows what else, he mused as he was forced to park way down the drive and walk up to the Hall.

The noise within was deafening, thump, thump, thump from some heavy metal band and Ross stopped in dismay at the sight of his father's rose bed where several cars had thoughtlessly driven over the miniature box hedge. *Peace* and *Ena Harkness* would never blossom again and the stone statue of Aphrodite with her urn was now urnless.

Ross was in a fury by the time he burst into the wide reception hall of his father's home, his home, too, till Jenna had driven him out. The sight sickened him. Paintings up the curving stairway were askew; there were glasses and empty wine bottles littering the antique furniture, drinks spilled, ashtrays overflowing when people had bothered to use them.

'Out!' he roared as he pulled the plug on Sweeney's mobile disco in the drawing room. 'I'll give you sixty seconds to get your stuff out of here!'

There had been confusion as Ross had stormed through the rest of the house, roaring at everyone to get out. There had been mumblings of, 'must be her father', 'bloody spoilsport', and worse, much, much worse.

In precisely seven minutes and thirty seconds the house had been cleared and every car and filthy van had departed in a convoy of belching petrol and diesel fumes. Ross, breathing steadily at last, had surveyed the damage to his father's beautiful home with dismay.

It would cost thousands to put back to rights but money wasn't the issue. He felt as if he himself had been vandalised. This was his home too, the place where he had grown up, it was a part of him and it had been trashed unmercifully.

He'd wandered the ground floor. In the study he picked up a Lalique glass ornament which his mother had bought his father on their honeymoon; a figurine of a dancer. She'd never pirouette again; a once graceful arm was smashed as if someone had used it to pry the top off a bottle of lager. Ross groaned and closed his eyes in despair. His father would be devastated.

Ross's anger had welled again then; a furious bubble of wrath against Jenna. How could she? How could she be so damned selfish and irresponsible as to let all this happen? And of course there was no sign of her which was typical of Jenna. When things got particularly difficult she ran for her life.

He found her at last. Down by the old thatched summerhouse in the grounds, swinging nonchalantly on the garden swing hanging from an oak tree. It had been there when he was a child and he had used it often. It was a place where one could be alone and think. He almost despised Jenna for using it now, as if she knew it had once been his special place and was trying to irritate him further.

The moon was bright and he could see her clearly. Backwards and forwards she swung, her clenched fists wrapped around the worn rope. Her red satin mini dress was hitched way up around her thighs, fully exposing her long tanned legs. Her feet were bare and dirty where she had raced across the gardens to get here. The bodice of the dress plunged so deeply at her cleavage that he wondered why she had bothered wearing the damned awful dress at all. It left nothing to the imagination.

She said nothing as he approached across the damp lawn but he heard her humming to herself; some blues number she often hummed or sung. Something about being nobody's child. Probably to irritate him further because she knew his musical taste was purely classical.

'Get off that swing, come back to the Hall with me and explain yourself, Jenna,' he'd said quietly and firmly, hanging onto his temper by a thread.

When she had laughed, he'd realised that was all he had expected of her. She slid off the swing, her bare feet slipped on the dewy grass and she giggled as he reached for her to save her from a fall. Clutching her hand tightly he'd hauled her back across the lawns to the house to make her face the damage and mayhem she had caused to his father's home.

He thrust her into the drawing room and turned on her, straining every muscle in his hard body to stop himself from putting her across his knee and giving her the spanking she should have had when she was four years old. But she was a grown woman now, in looks if not in mind.

'When the hell are you going to grow up?' he seethed at her. 'This is your eighteenth birthday not your eighth! Look at the damage here, just look at it Jenna! Proud, are you? Have you no decency and respect for other peoples' lives and property? How dare you do this in my father's house. How dare you open up his house to such filth and depravation. How dare you!'

Nothing. No regrets, no apologies. Nothing from the wild child. She stood leaning against the Georgian side table next to the fireplace where logs still smouldered, swirling her index finger in a pool of alcohol, staring at the design she was making. Then slowly she had lifted her head, her thick raven hair curtaining one side of her tilted face, her smoky grey eyes sparkling with insolence. Her full mouth had curved into a small smile and she had spoken at last, words that to this day he didn't understand.

'At last I have roused you,' she murmured silkily.

Ross stared at her, not understanding, but that was nothing new where she was concerned. They were poles apart in every way.

'Yes, inflamed me, Jenna. I am fit to burst with indignation,' he barked at her. 'You are nothing but a spoilt brat. So your mother couldn't make it back from Paris for your birthday and this is your revenge. Invite the world's wasters to wreak havoc on my father's home —'

'I didn't invite them!' she suddenly burst out defensively. 'A friend rang to wish me a happy birthday and was dismayed to find I was on my own in this...this mausoleum you call home, and she organised the party before I could stop her. I am not spoilt. And besides, now that you are here, making me feel bad about something I was helpless to do anything against, let me remind you that this is *my* home too!'

She paused to take a full breath, her chest heaving with emotion. 'But not by choice,' she went on heatedly. 'I've always hated it here. I've never belonged. I wanted my own place but they wouldn't let me! Everyone pushes me around –'

'Your mother and Alastair care about you –'

'My friends care but my family don't!' she shrieked, trembling with rage. 'It's my birthday and they aren't here. They are having a fun time in Paris and I was left here on my own!'

Immediately Ross's heart went out to her. Yes, she should be spending the night with her family, but the bare facts were that no one was here for her.

'I'm here,' he told her softly but even as the words slid from his lips he knew it would be no consolation to her.

'Huh! But not by choice! Your father ordered you to be here and you, being the obedient son without a mind of your own, just jump when he whistles,' she taunted, lifting her trembling chin defiantly. 'Well I don't jump for *anyone*. I'm glad my friends organised a party and –'

'And Jenna gets what she wants at everyone's expense!' Ross retaliated sharply, infuriated at her taunt that he hadn't a mind of his own. Guilt too fanned his rage because she was right in one respect; he wouldn't be here if his father hadn't requested him to be.

'I never get anything I want, Ross. I get pushed from pillar to post to fit in with everyone else's lives –'

'Oh, for goodness sake, Jenna, you would see that you have it all if you cared to open your eyes and look around you. And I needn't have come at all. I could have stayed in London and ignored you but I didn't. Happy Birthday!' he sighed in exasperation.

'I bet you didn't even know it was my birthday till tonight,' she accused knowingly and Ross's conscience burned. 'So where's my present then?' she taunted further, hands defiantly planted on her narrow hips. Her grey eyes glittered triumphantly, guessing, wrongly as it happened, that he hadn't brought her anything.

Annoyed at her selfishness his hand had gone to his pocket and before he was fully aware of what he was doing he had thrown the small but precious package at her. It caught her on the shoulder and her eyes widened with a childlike fear that had shaken him to the roots. As her complexion paled from flushed with anger to white with fright he thought she might pass out.

The sight of her, pale and trembling, so very fragile and vulnerable, had drained Ross's fury instantly and he had gone to her. Wide eyed and fearful she had flinched as he stopped in front of her. Their eyes locked for an instant, both unsure of what was going to happen next and then suddenly her head had bent and she started to sob and he reached for her; wanting to hold her sad little body hard against his to comfort her.

'I'm sorry, darling,' he heard himself saying thickly. Not his own voice at all. 'Forgive me, I've frightened you. Forgive me...' he added roughly and passionately.

And she sobbed even more and clung to him and he had held her tightly, nuzzling her perfumed hair and breathing the musky scent deeply.

Then it had happened; the stirring inside him. His head reeled as he recognised the punch of arousal deep in his groin. It shocked him deeply that it was Jenna who was arousing the passion in him and for a moment his body tensed in alarm. He felt her hot wet face against the relative coolness of his; the trembling slimness of her heated body through the satin that barely covered it. Before he knew what he was doing he found himself lifting her chin to look deeply into her misty grey eyes, brimming with tears, which seemed to be pleading for him to do something.

And in confusion he had answered that unspoken plea in the only way he felt possible at the time; his mouth hungrily seeking hers, wanting to make it all right for her, wanting to make it right for himself, *just damned well wanting her.*

She had responded so passionately, so urgently that his breath caught in his throat with shock. Shock for himself at the way he was feeling, out of control, and shock for her blatant wantonness as their mouths grated hard together.

The world had spiralled at these new feelings which had so suddenly erupted inside him; the need to be with her so completely, the need to possess her in the most primeval way. Jenna was now wild in a very different way – wild for him and it stunned him. Her need was apparently as deep as his and yet, through the haze of shock at their sudden sexual awareness, he thought this was the first time he had really understood her insecurity. Jenna, so wild and misunderstood, wanting love so very badly and the world letting her down.

In the heat of their passion, not thinking any more, not caring, they had tumbled to the rug and their kisses had blazed the way to a mounting passion he had never felt before or since. She was fire in his arms, clutching at him and gasping his name, hot and wild and yet warm and sensuous. Such a mixture of muddled passion, such a firebrand of erotica.

Her small, perfect breasts thrust against his caresses and then his mouth as he drew on her sweetness, dizzy with feeling for her, loving her in that crazy moment with a fervour that had shaken his whole life.

Nothing could stop them. Not the phone ringing in the background, not the sudden spark of flame from the tired smouldering logs behind them, not the thud of their hearts warning them. Nothing could stop the heated flow of need and desire that rampaged through them like an out-of-control forest fire.

She was moist for him, hot and moist and his breathing was ragged with passion as she flowered for him where his fingers caressed between her legs. And then he was fumbling with his clothes, powered by an urgency that made him feel dizzy with its intensity. And suddenly they were both deeply aroused and he was thrusting into her, wanting her so desperately he would have died of it.

Cutting through their fevered kisses she cried out his name, an impassioned, plaintive cry, and his whole body froze over her as if something had struck him from behind. His head reeled with the realisation that he was her first lover, the shock so immense because it had never crossed his mind that such a wild child-woman could still be...and then her kisses were more ardent, encouraging him; her words almost incoherent but urging him on nonetheless.

'Oh, don't stop, my Ross, my love. So...so long, so long to wait and please...please don't stop.'

She clung to him, arching her hips at him, wrapping her legs around him, brushing kisses across his face and neck and he hadn't been able to stop his total possession of her. *Nothing* could have stopped him. He burned as if in the throes of a fever. Together they had moved, as one, as if it had always been meant to be, Jenna and Ross, Ross and Jenna. Mouths greedy and possessive, bodies hot and demanding, wanting every part of each other, wanting to be bonded together for evermore.

He had loved her so utterly and completely; kissing her willing mouth so ardently, holding her and caressing her and thrusting into her till their climax rose heatedly. Higher and higher they soared in painful ecstasy till at last they broke and burst forth, liquid fire of such deep intensity that they both shook as if electrified when the precious moment came.

And then, exhausted and trembling after the release of such unbridled need, she had cried in his arms. Her thin arms clinging to him like a vine against the hard wall of his hot body, she had cried as if her heart would break. And he had held her so fiercely and possessively and wanted to cry too; a plaintive roar for forgiveness for not being stronger and holding back from her.

The fire in the hearth had finally died by the time their heartbeats had slowed. Jenna still clung to him, weak and senseless now. She was soft and limp and sated and he held her, smoothing her tousled hair with tender strokes, not sure what to do or say as his head cleared and the enormity of what had happened became a guilty reality.

At last he brushed a tender kiss across her dewy brow and then gently lifted her up from the rug. Still clinging to him she nuzzled her face into his neck and he carried her upstairs and along the landing to her bedroom where he carefully laid her down on her bed.

She was asleep as he pulled the downy duvet up around her chin and he had stood for a long time looking down on her. Her long black lashes, sooty and caked with too much mascara rested on her silky cheeks; a wisp of jet black hair was caught at the corner of her moist, swollen lips. He had carefully brushed back the errant strand and she had murmured softly at the small intrusion into her trancelike state. His heart had torn at the look of vulnerability on her beautiful face.

Was this the real Jenna? Was all the rest the bravado and attention seeking of a troubled young woman with a muddled past? Perhaps for the first time he was beginning to realise her complexity. She was so confused, so in need of love and care and after her urgency with him tonight it seemed he was the one she wanted to offer it all to her.

He had worked into the small hours clearing up the mess after the party. The effort a panacea for his conscience. He told himself a thousand times that he shouldn't have let it happen. And as dawn broke after a sleepless night in his suite of rooms along the passageway from Jenna's bedroom he came to the final conclusion that it had happened because it had been inevitable.

His fury had finally snapped the pattern of their uneasy relationship. And it was because of this astonishing realisation, that there was a fine line between hate and love, that he hadn't been able to go to her bed for the rest of the night. It would have been so easy to crawl in beside her and hold her to him but the inevitable would have happened.

He couldn't make love to her again, not without resolving their feelings for each other with words. Enough damage had been done already by blatant sexual need. He couldn't allow himself to let go like that again. It had been impetuous, dangerous, completely out of character for him. Softly, softly from now on. Because Jenna had a fragile heart.

Ross got up the next morning and showered and dressed before making coffee and taking it up to Jenna's room. A new day and a new beginning and they needed to talk. He was still deeply shocked by what he had allowed to happen, and bemused by the depth of his feelings for her. She would be confused too and would need handling with tenderness and loving care and they would sensibly talk it through and decide what to do about their future together.

She was sitting at her dressing table when he opened the bedroom door, balancing the tray on one hand. She was fully dressed in tight jeans and a soft pink sweater, looking at her scrubbed face in the mirror as if seeing herself for the first time.

He remembered thinking at the time how beautiful and yet vulnerable she looked; the wild child sucked out from her and gone forever. She'd become a woman now and all because of him. His heart had clenched with emotion as he put the tray down and went and stood behind her, too nervous to reach out and touch her.

They looked at each other in the mirror and he knew he would be the first to speak because her eyes seemed to demand it. They were wide and unsure and he wanted to put her at ease, but what to say and how to say it was something else. This was something so very new to him, so unexpected in his normally orderly life that for once he was the one feeling vulnerable.

'Darling, I can't begin to tell you how sorry I am,' he started softly. And he wanted to go on and say more; that, in a way, he was glad it had happened because it made the future clearer for them. But she didn't give him the chance.

Her eyes narrowed and their expression changed from plaintive and unsure to steely determination. She swung round on her dressing table stool and shot to her feet.

'Sorry!' she breathed indignantly, her body tense. 'I don't want to hear sorry!'

'It's a start, Jenna,' he offered gently, 'It's the only explanation I can come up with for what happened last night. It was wonderful but we need to talk it through.'

'What's wrong with you, Ross?' she spat. 'Can't you bring yourself to come up with more than just a feeble apology for this apparently *wonderful* happening?'

She was hurt and Ross recognised the hurt. He didn't want her hurt and on the defensive again. He reached for her, to take her in his arms and reassure her that it was going to be all right, but she stepped back. Her chin came up, her fists clenched and inwardly Ross wondered why he had thought the wild child had gone from her. Was she ashamed of what had happened? Facing him now in the cold light of day was she seeing the folly of their lovemaking and regretting it bitterly? Had he got it all wrong in thinking that she must feel the same way as he?

'I don't want to see you hurt, Jenna,' he started again. 'We need to talk and –'

She bit her lower lip and stepped even further back from him, edging around the dressing table.

'Why?' she breathed hotly. 'We've never talked before. Why now? Because you made love to me last night doesn't give you any rights. And you couldn't hurt me if you came at me with a razor-edged sabre. I don't want your apologies or your regrets for what happened –'

'I don't regret what happened; I'm sorry yes but not regretful,' he tried to reassure her,' and I hope you don't regret it either because –'

'Because it was hopeless, wasn't it?' she murmured plaintively, still backing off from him till she came up against the edge of her bed. 'Because if it hadn't been, you would have been in this bed with me this morning when I woke up, holding me, but you weren't because you'd got what you wanted and a repeat –'

'Jenna, please,' Ross ground out. 'Listen to me and you'll realise what I'm trying to say.'

'I hear you well enough, Ross, and I understand perfectly,' she cried hotly. 'Last night was last night and this...this morning it's different and no...' she fumbled, 'no it isn't different. It's the same as it always was. I was never *anyone* in your ordered life. You still hate me and I hate you, Ross, more so now because of what you did to me last night!'

He'd inwardly flinched at her words and her anger but he couldn't retaliate with the accusation that it takes two to tango. God, she had been more than willing and if she had said one negative word he would have stopped. But dammit, she hadn't. And now, now she was back to being the wild child, full of loathing for him, blaming him.

And what a fool he had been through the night, believing that she must feel the same depth of emotion for him as he felt for her. He had been used that was all, as her bonus birthday gift. She had gained his ultimate submission, his complete vulnerability, just as she had planned.

He stared at her, blanking off all the new-found feelings that he had finally acknowledged as dawn had broken. He crushed the love inside him, as she gave him one last, coldly hostile glance from her smoky eyes. And then, with a dismissive toss of her head, she had crossed the room to the wardrobe and hauled out a leather jacket.

'Get real, Ross Cameron,' she advised stiffly, without looking at him again. 'I'm sorry, too, for last night because you caught me out in a moment of weakness and you weren't worth it. You were the worst lover I've ever had!' With that she had stormed from the room, slamming the bedroom door hard behind her.

Her words cut right through to his very soul. Though he knew he was the only lover she had ever had, it didn't help. He stood stiffly in her bedroom, waiting for the slam of the huge oak door downstairs and when it came he breathed raggedly at last.

God, what a fool he had been. She had used him and he had misinterpreted all that had happened in the depth of their passion; believed it to be equally meaningful for them both.

What madness! She was right. Nothing had changed between them. And now she had left him with something worse to live with: bloody guilt for what he had passionately taken from her. Her wild childhood.

It had festered like a poison ever since.

And it was coming to a head now, Ross realised as he opened his eyes and blinked out of the car window to see the Patersons building towering into a matt-grey sky before him.

'We're here, Sir.'

Wearily Ross reached for his mobile phone. His whole body was stiff with exhaustion after his painful reverie into the past.

'Take me home, Anthony,' he instructed his chauffeur as he punched out the number of Patersons to reschedule the meeting he couldn't face now. And Karen – he would ring her too, to cancel their dinner date. 'Then hang around while I pack and drive me to the airport. I have a meeting in Paris to attend,' he concluded wearily.

So the decision was made. He was going to Jenna – and God help him because the decision to face that guilt ridden past of his, might be the worst of his life, but it was inevitable all the same. He had probably known it from the moment his father had asked for his help to stop Jenna's wedding.

Ross frowned as the car purred him homewards. What his father couldn't know was that to see Jenna married, to whoever she chose, was his son's dearest wish. When she was committed to another man Ross would be free of her at last. So why was he even bothering going to Paris at all when he wanted this marriage for her?

To finally lay the ghost of her damned eighteenth birthday, that was why!

chapter three

'You wouldn't dare, Jenna,' Paloma laughed incredulously. 'You look ravishing in it but it's not suitable as a wedding dress. You'll cause an uproar.'

'It's going to be a very private ceremony,' Jenna told her friend over her shoulder as she surveyed the dress critically in the full-length mirror.

'Mademoiselle is shopping for a wedding dress?' the sales adviser suddenly gasped breathlessly, wringing her hands in anguish. 'But this is not suitable as your friend has said. This is for cocktails and not for a wedding!'

The assistant looked distraught at having misinterpreted her customer's needs and hovered worriedly as Jenna twirled in front of the gilt framed mirror in the exclusive designer dress shop along the Champs Elysee.

The burgundy-coloured silk dress clung where it touched and swirled from below the knee to the ankle. The back dipped down to the waist and the high front was encrusted with oyster pearl beads in a floral design that snaked down one side to the waist.

Yes, it was a cocktail dress and Jenna knew it but what she saw in the reflection of the mirror wasn't the rather bizarre dress with a price tag on it that would have lesser mortals screaming with terror. What she saw was frothy white lace and satin with miles of tulle flowing from the waist, a train that would take at least three small nieces, if she had any, to keep in control. Her long jet hair would be ribboned with spirals of white satin and her face would be flushed with love and happiness.

She saw in her fantasy what she had secretly dreamed of most of her life: security and a picture book wedding with the man she loved and who loved her. And the life that followed; a happy and fulfilled marriage without the pitfalls her mother had suffered in her three marriages.

But it was a fantasy and she knew it, and life wasn't picture-book and dreamy. Life was mostly a compromise as she knew to her cost.

'Mademoiselle,' the assistant said under her breath, 'this dress is beautiful but *not* a wedding dress,' she insisted.

Jenna forced a small reassuring smile for the unfortunate assistant who was getting more embarrassed by the second.

'But I'm marrying an unconventional artist, Madame,' Jenna explained lightly.

'She's marrying Marcel DeLuc,' Paloma cheekily offered to the bemused assistant whose expression suddenly switched to wide eyed awe. Everyone in Paris had heard of Marcel DeLuc.

Jenna turned back to the mirror and smoothed her trembling hands over her slender hips. 'Marcel will love it,' she murmured to herself and added ruefully, 'if he ever notices.'

Lifting her small chin she took one last look at herself in the mirror and defiantly stated, 'I'll take it,' and swept back to the opulent changing room where she stripped off the inappropriate dress and flung it across the back of a pale-pink club chair and glared at it so hard she forced tears to her eyes.

She wanted to weep for herself but she didn't because she had learned control now. It was all bottled up inside her, unable to get out because it hurt so much. The dress was a damned joke and her whole life had been a joke since....

Jenna swallowed her tears and slid into her own clothes – a short skirted black Chanel suit – slid a comb through her long bob and glared at her reflection in a wall mirror. She knew what she was doing. She was going to marry Marcel and it would work because they both wanted it to work. It was time for her to settle down and put the past behind her. She was determined to do just that. Lay Ross to rest and give Marcel her best.

Jenna was slicking more gloss to her lips when Paloma opened the door and poked her blonde head around it.

'I've ordered a taxi. We'll lunch at Max's. OK?'

'Of course,' Jenna grinned. 'I'm starving and I would love a glass of wine.'

'Good girl. Hurry up then I'm weak with hunger.'

Jenna sighed as she rummaged in her handbag for her credit card to pay for the dress. The thought of food made her feel sick but she had promised Paloma lunch and, next to good looking men, Paloma had a taste for good looking food too!

Paloma was the closest friend Jenna had ever had; the daughter of a wealthy family from Barcelona. They had met at an exclusive college in Lyon; Paloma taking a social studies degree and Jenna reading the history of art. She'd just completed her degree course with great success but since meeting Marcel had put a career on hold till after the wedding. Before returning to Barcelona to take another degree, Paloma was staying with her in Paris for a few days and they were shopping and gossiping, both of which Jenna was tiring of now.

She loved Paloma dearly but keeping up the pretence of being a happy bride was beginning to take its toll on her nerves. Paloma was leaving the following morning however so all she had to do was to keep a smile on her face for just a short while longer.

Ten minutes later they leapt out of the taxi outside Max's and Jenna blinked as a photographer snapped them both as they went through the front doors of the fashionable restaurant.

'You've got a lifetime of this to come: paparazzi at every turn,' Paloma grumbled light-heartedly as they were shown to their seats by an attentive waiter. 'I don't know how you are going to bear it.'

'They'll soon lose interest,' Jenna stated optimistically. 'Of course if Gerard DeLuc gets to be President it might be different, but I'll face that if it happens. I'm marrying an artist, not a prospective president's son.'

'What's he like, the father-in-law-to-be?' Paloma asked as she eagerly took the menu from the waiter and scanned it hungrily.

Jenna told her absently. 'Ambitious. I've only met him the once, here in Paris. He was very busy and he treated me with indifference.'

'Is it cold at this table for Mademoiselle?' the waiter asked with concern as Jenna suddenly shivered.

She smiled and fluttered her thick black lashes at him. 'No, it's perfect,' she murmured.

Ross Cameron... Speaking of Gerard DeLuc's indifference had reminded her of Ross's. Gerard had looked at her in the same way as Ross always had. As if she might as well be part of the furniture for all he cared.

And suddenly Jenna had even less appetite than she had before. She ordered anyway; some clams she could toy with on her plate and a glass of white wine. Paloma ordered, something from every course and Jenna knew the lunch was going to be a long one.

'I wish I could have met him this trip, Jenna,' Paloma sighed wistfully. 'Never mind. I'll meet him soon enough at the wedding.'

'Who?' Jenna asked absently.

'Marcel of course,' Paloma laughed. 'Honestly, Jenna, you're miles away.'

Jenna grinned. She needed to concentrate harder. 'Yes, Marcel will be sorry to hear he missed you. Funny, but he's in Spain at the moment, the Guggenheim Museum in Bilbao.'

'Oh, Jenna, you are going to have such an exciting life with your new husband. Travelling the world, meeting such fascinating people. I guess that is why your mother is so reticent about the wedding. She's really going to miss you.'

So Paloma had noticed her mother's withdrawn attitude towards Jenna's engagement. Jenna frowned. Yes there had been tension between her and her mother since she had announced that she was going to marry Marcel. Though they didn't always see eye to eye, generally they could work things out. But Yvonne's attitude had confused her. First had come the explosion of fury and then...then nothing but a sort of tight-lipped apathy that had been worse than another full blown row. It seemed Yvonne was burying her head in the sand over it all and this was deeply upsetting to Jenna.

'She hasn't even met him yet: refuses too,' Jenna muttered ruefully. She sighed and stared into her wine glass. 'She said the gossip in the newspapers is enough for her and she doesn't want to meet him. But she's going to have to once we agree the wedding day and the venue.'

Paloma shifted uncomfortably. 'I didn't know they hadn't met,' she said worriedly.

'It's not a problem. She'll come round in the end,' Jenna shrugged dismissively.

Perhaps Paloma was right and her mother was going to miss her but it was probably truer to say that Yvonne was fearful of her daughter making a wrong marriage as she herself had done, frequently. But if only her mother would open her heart to her so she would truly know how she felt about the marriage. To say she didn't approve because of Marcel's reputation just wasn't enough.

Although Jenna was sure she was doing the right thing she would have liked her mother's approval; but Yvonne's lack of communication wasn't helpful at all.

But when had her mother been any different? Her first marriage to Jenna's father, whom Jenna had never known, was a taboo subject and never spoken of. The second to... Jenna refused to think about that one anymore. She'd quite successfully blocked it out over the years, her mother too.

Jenna bit down hard on her lower lip and leaned back as the waiter brought her clams and Paloma's first course, a dish of mussels in a bubbling sauce.

And then Alastair. Well Alastair Cameron, too, had been a disaster in the end, but Jenna knew her mother still kept in contact with him, still hoped that one day a miracle might happen and they would be reconciled.

That was the difference between mother and daughter. Jenna didn't believe in miracles. Hard facts were her bible. Alastair had let her mother go. Just like that.

And Ross had come from the same mould as his father. He had allowed her to walk out on him that morning after her disastrous birthday party and that was proof that he hadn't cared either. If he had, if his heart had beat as sincerely as hers that night, he wouldn't have let her walk away so easily the next morning.

Far safer to compromise; build a future on a determination to succeed and lay to rest the deceptive ghost of love for good and all. Once married to Marcel she'd be too busy to dwell on the past.

Jenna sipped her wine pensively and watched Paloma enjoying her food. Her dear, dear friend didn't know about Ross, the man she had loved all her life, all the life since he had come into it. He'd bowled her over with his good looks and his quiet sophistication. He was so damned English, so cool, and so charismatic. She had always wanted to get under his skin, to find the real man beneath, and she had, briefly, and he was all she had hoped him to be. Passionate, exciting and... and then, nothing!

She reflected that Ross had driven the wild child out of her and yet in a way he had been the cause of her wilful ways in the first place. Being young and naive she hadn't known how to handle her feelings for him. She had fought him out of sheer frustration at the way he treated her: that blind indifference that had boiled within her until she had always, but always snapped.

But he never lost his cool. He was always so in control...but once... Her head still swam at the memory, her stomach still clenched violently at the reminder of his complete possession of her that night. Body and soul in one hasty coupling that had devastated her with its power. It had shocked and excited her and later confused her and deeply hurt her.

'Aren't you eating?' Paloma enquired.

Suddenly Jenna smoothed her brow with the tips of her fingers and forced a smile for Paloma. 'Yes of course.' She picked up a fork and prodded a clam.

'You must remember to give me your wedding list before I leave in the morning.' Paloma lifted her head to look at her friend. 'You have done one, haven't you?'

'Well actually, no,' Jenna admitted. 'I was rather hoping my mother might help me out on that one.'

'Well I think it's about time you and your mother got this wedding sorted, Jenna,' Paloma reproached. 'You have the dress at least but you haven't even set the date yet. I'm beginning to wonder if this wedding is going to happen at all.'

'It's going to happen, of that I'm certain,' Jenna

smiled. She was never more certain of anything in her life.

'I'll order the stainless steel saucepans then,' Paloma grinned.

'Don't you dare!' Jenna laughed. 'If you imagine for a minute I'm going to cook once I'm married, think again!'

'Can't wait to try on all my new clothes,' Paloma laughed as later they bundled all the packages into a cab and slumped into the back.

Jenna clutched the boxed silk cocktail dress on her lap as the taxi wove its way through the congested Paris traffic and wondered what her mother would think of it. She could almost anticipate Yvonne's reaction to the rather bizarre choice. Her eyes might widen but that would be about it. Why was her mother treating it as if this wedding wasn't happening? It wasn't as if Marcel was a poor artist, and his family background was impeccable. Most mothers would be delighted their daughter was marrying into such a good family.

The girls entered the wide hallway of the elegant third floor apartment overlooking the Seine, chatting over their shopping expedition and brushing raindrops from their hair. They were greeted by Chantelle, the maid, who held up her fingers to shush them both.

'Madame has a client with her,' she warned them. 'But not in the studio. They are both in the salon.'

Jenna nodded, knowing her mother didn't like to be disturbed when she was involved with a client. Yvonne had picked up the threads of the interior design business she had left behind when Alastair had come into her life and was much in demand for her advice and services once again.

Jenna heard the muted tones of conversation coming from the salon and frowned slightly. Paloma had just hurled herself upstairs to try on her new outfits, Chantelle had departed to the kitchen to wait for instructions on tea for the client and Jenna was alone in the hallway.

Alone with her heart thudding perilously. The accents coming from the drawing room were English, not French. Her mother's clients were always French.

Jenna stared wildly at the curtain-draped double French doors of the room, stiff with shock, unable to move a muscle. She knew that voice, that soft timbred, almost expressionless tone that didn't rise or fall with emotion because the speaker was always too damned cool.

This couldn't be. This couldn't be happening. This was a nightmare!

chapter four

Ross Cameron stood up abruptly and turned towards the doors as they flew open, so violently that each door thumped against the ornate occasional chairs flanking the opening. Yvonne pale and anguished-looking, shot to her feet and clutched her hands tensely together.

Jenna stood in the doorway and, at the sight of Ross, her breath caught in her throat. Her right hand flew, instinctively, to the pendant she always wore at her throat and the tips of her fingers agitatedly twirled the drop pearl. A nervous reaction to the shock of her suspicions being confirmed by sight of the last person on earth she had expected to see. She had inwardly prayed that she might be wrong and the cool tones she had heard were not Ross's. But they were. He was here, right here in her home and looking at her now with the usual contempt he seemed only to reserve for her.

Her wide smoky eyes flicked apprehensively from Ross to her mother. She felt as if the walls were closing in on her in a silent vice, crushing her heart into a molten ball. Why was he here? Had something happened...to Alastair!

Ross was the first to move. Slowly, lazily, he came towards her across the cream coloured Aubusson rug to where she still stood in the doorway, unable to move a single muscle of her slight body.

He was the same as he had always been, tall, breathtakingly good-looking, elegant, impeccably dressed in a very British way; a three piece suit of severe navy with a very fine grey thread through it, a crisp white shirt and a conventionally patterned grey silk tie. He was perfectly turned out, hair sleek and glossy, unruffled by travel.

She couldn't take her bleak gaze from his handsome face and her heart stilled apprehensively. His mouth was straining into a smile, not one of pleasure at sight of her but one of polite formality. His greeting and words were perfunctory. He kissed the air at each side of her cheeks and spoke softly. 'Jenna, how lovely to see you.'

Nothing more, nothing less and then he was turning away from her, putting air and space between them as he strode back to the marble fireplace to rejoin Yvonne who was watching them both with eyes wide and slightly glassy.

Something *had* happened to Alastair? Otherwise why were both looking so grave? Her heart came to life and started thudding fearfully.

Jenna worked her mouth into a semblance of words that came out in an anxious husky whisper. 'It's Alastair, isn't it? What's happened?'

Both looked at her in astonishment, as if neither were sure the concerned query had actually emanated from her lips.

Yvonne broke the silence that followed her daughter's surprisingly anguished question.

'Alastair is well, Jenna. He sends his very best regards,' Yvonne murmured as she reached for the bell-ring at the side of the fireplace. 'We will have tea now.

Give Chantelle instructions, would you Jenna? And...and then come and join us. Will Paloma be coming down for tea?'

Still in shock at Ross being here in this very room with them, Jenna couldn't help the retort that came from her pale lips.

'Of course. She is our guest. Why shouldn't she be joining us?'

At the slight flickering of Ross's eyes at her abrasive remark to her mother, Jenna could have bitten her tongue off. Instead she bit her lip remorsefully for not having more control over her mouth. But the sight of him, so completely unexpected in the run up time to her wedding day, had had that effect on her, swinging her dizzily back to her wild childhood when she had never bothered to think before she spoke.

'Paloma is Jenna's friend from college and is staying for a few days. She'll be going back to Spain tomorrow but returning for...for the...the wedding,' Yvonne explained nervously to Ross as she sank back down into the sofa that stretched in front of the pale cream marble fireplace. With her back to Yvonne now Jenna couldn't see her mothers face but she could see her long artistic fingers come up to rub the bridge of her nose worriedly.

So her mother had told Ross she was going to be married. Jenna's heart clenched tightly at the thought of how that news might have affected him. In her wildest thoughts she imagined his face darkening with fury and jealousy, but sadly reality was what she was seeing now: that same cold indifference.

So what had Ross come for and why was her mother obviously so stressed out over it?

Jenna turned and left the room hurriedly for the kitchen to give Chantelle her instructions; tea for four in the salon. At a lesser pace she went back along the corridor, drawing breath and trying to recover her equilibrium. She was dismayed to feel her hands trembling and she clenched them tightly before stepping back into the room, aware of an awkward atmosphere and just catching the last words Ross was saying to her mother.

'I don't see what this has to do with my father or me, Yvonne. I only came because you asked...' he had left the sentence unfinished because she had come back into the room.

Jenna clenched her fists at her side as she stepped further into the room, heading for the wing chair on the other side of the wide fireplace, as far from Ross as was possible. Her heart staggered at what she had overheard; his tone showing his obvious reluctance to be here and his words implying that Yvonne had requested the visit. But she could have been wrong in that supposition. She was still in shock and perhaps not hearing clearly.

'So Alastair is well,' she bravely started as she flung herself into the chair, kicking off her elegant high heels and coiling her long legs up on to the seat beside her. No one else was saying anything and the sudden silence was uncomfortable and she needed to fill it. 'I'm pleased to hear it. So why this sudden visit, Ross?' she asked with a smile, striving to sound normal though she was feeling far from it.

They both spoke at once, Ross and Yvonne. In the confusion Jenna thought her mother had said, 'I asked him,' but then Ross's deep timbred voice had taken precedence.

'I'm passing through Paris on business and thought I would look you both up and see how you are.'

His eyes didn't hold Jenna's long enough after he spoke for her to be convinced that was the truth. She had a horrible sinking feeling in the pit of her stomach that it was a lie and what her mother had said was the truth; she had asked him to come. But why?

'Ross will be staying for a few days,' her mother continued and Jenna's breath caught in her throat and her fingernails dug into her legs.

It was the very last thing on earth she wanted. She had just come to the biggest decision of her life; to marry, to clear the backlog of her past and start a new life as a wife. She didn't want Ross, of all people, here to complicate that decision. Why, oh, why had he come now? It just wasn't fair!

It took all the strength in her body to force words from her lips. She tried to sound nonchalant as she spoke, as if she wasn't completely thrown by his presence.

'That will be nice,' she lied. She lifted her chin. 'You must come back for the wedding too. When we've fixed a date we'll send you an invitation.'

The thought was abhorrent to her; Ross witnessing her marriage to Marcel but she knew he would refuse because why should he accept? She was nothing to him and time out of Ross's business world for even five minutes worth of her life wasn't even a remote possibility.

But the offer appeared to have stunned Ross and her

mother. The silence was suddenly heavier than the strained atmosphere. Jenna felt compelled to break it.

'Well why not?' she heard herself reason, in a voice that sounded as if it was echoing down a long tunnel. 'I suppose you could call yourself the closest thing to family we've got. Come to think of it you could give me away. That's if you can fit me into your busy schedule. I'm sure Alastair won't put himself out to find the time to –'

'That's enough, Jenna!' her mother suddenly cried and got to her feet. 'I'll help Chantelle with the tea,' she said shortly. And refusing to meet anyone's gaze she swept out of the room wafting Diorissimo into the air as she made her hasty exit.

Jenna rubbed her forehead, wishing it was possible to suck back the bitchy words she had just spoken so thoughtlessly and upset her mother with. Any reminder that Alastair put business before pleasure was hurtful to her mother. Lazily fixing her smoky gaze onto an embarrassed-looking Ross she shrugged her shoulders helplessly. No point in apologising to him, it was her mother she had hurt and later she would make it up to her.

'Something I said?' she asked with simpering sarcasm.

Ross looked at her coldly for a very long time. A glacial gaze that Jenna was able to bear because it all came flooding back to her: past bitter confrontations with him. She'd borne that look before and probably would till the end of time.

At last Ross shook his head and dropped his gaze from her to the thick carpet at his feet. His voice dripped censorship when he spoke. 'My father said you had mellowed and I disputed the statement and I was right. You haven't changed a bit, Jenna.'

He lifted his dark head then and she met his cold look bravely though she inwardly squirmed at her own bad behaviour: confirmation to him that she was exactly the same as she had always been.

'I haven't seen your father for three years,' she said quietly. 'How would he know anything about my life now?'

'Alastair and Yvone speak regularly on the phone as you well know. They handle their separation in a civilised way,' he told her stiffly, as if implying she was incapable of handling anything in a civilised fashion. 'Yvonne also said that you had mellowed, though where she got the idea from I can't imagine.'

'She knows me better than anyone,' Jenna replied tightly. 'Anyway, whether I have mellowed or not is irrelevant. What is far more interesting is why you are here. I'm sure your number-crunching has brought you to Paris before now but you have never called on us, so why now?'

'I hear you have a degree,' Ross said, looking past her to the long windows where rain was still pattering lightly on the floor-to-ceiling panes.

He couldn't even look her in the eye. Jenna crossly let a small explosion of air out through her pursed lips. 'Don't tell me you've come all this way to congratulate me,' she said. 'A fax would have sufficed.'

He looked at her then, as coldly as ever. His equally cold words struck her icily. 'I'm trying to make conversation, Jenna,' he told her. 'If your years of studying haven't taught you to read between the lines then I fear it was all a waste of time, degree or not.'

'Still as pompous as ever, Ross,' Jenna cut back. 'You certainly haven't got yourself a life since last I saw you. You always were reticent in coming forward. I asked you a question which you have evaded with an obscure enquiry about my degree. It suggests you have something to hide: obviously your reasons for being here.'

She thought she saw a small cynical smile play at the corner of his mouth but it didn't last long enough for her to be sure.

'I'm a man of few unnecessary words, as you must realise by now.'

She smiled ruefully. 'You contradict yourself, Ross. You've just brought up my education which was totally unnecessary. How am I to be expected to read between the lines of your banal conversation when I never have understood you?'

They stared at each other bleakly, the silence interminable again; the years and years of harsh verbal exchanges coming back to haunt them both. Nothing had changed between them. They were still hostile to each other. Jenna wished with all her heart that Paloma would burst into the room and cavort for them in her latest purchases and so ease this bleak tension.

Which was exactly what happened. If only other wishes could so easily be granted Jenna mused forlornly as she stood up as Paloma stepped into the room, about to twirl in a stunning red Dolce & Gabbana suit which set off her lush blonde hair and her pale but creamy complexion.

Paloma stopped dead at the sight of Ross standing stiffly by the fireplace and Jenna noted the slight change in her colouring which she knew from old indicated that Paloma's hormones were rising to the surface of her skin. Paloma was deeply impressed by the sight of Ross's tall elegant sophistication in front of her. She smiled, a very interested smile that would leave any man but Ross Cameron in no doubt that she was interested in every sense. But Ross was too cold hearted to respond to Paloma's flirting. He looked at her blankly.

'Oh, you have a visitor,' Paloma murmured seductively and brazenly stepped towards him. Jenna just managed to get the introductions in before she grasped his hand enthusiastically.

'Ross is a family friend,' Jenna ended quickly after deciding that a fuller explanation wouldn't be digested as already Paloma was looking as if the stars had fallen out of the heavenly skies and scattered at her feet. She positively twinkled with delight as she took Ross's outstretched hand and held on to it far longer than was decent.

Jenna was further put out when Ross responded to Paloma in fluent Spanish. He said he was pleased to meet her, asked where her family came from and yes, he'd been to Barcelona many times and thought it a very buzzy city; and wasn't it unusual that she was so fair-haired for a Spaniard. To which Paloma replied that in many regions of her country fair hair was the norm and they both laughed until Jenna wanted to scream.

Paloma fluttered her eyelashes a lot and Ross, damn him to hell and back, was enjoying it! She couldn't ever remember a time when Ross had talked to her so enthusiastically, hung on to *her* every word. It hurt, horribly and she didn't want it to. Damn it she didn't want to feel anything where he was concerned.

'I must go and change,' Paloma laughed at last. 'Tea must be nearly ready and I'd hate to spill anything on my new outfit.' She twirled suddenly, fully aware of her gorgeous figure, her lovely legs. 'It suits me well, doesn't it Ross?' she fluttered for a compliment and Jenna wanted the ground to open under her friend.

'A very nice girl,' Ross commented after Paloma had sashayed out of the room. 'So natural and unpretentious for a girl who comes from one of the most important banking families in Barcelona.'

Jenna uncomfortably realised that Paloma had just done something she had never achieved, cracked Ross's tough shell enough to make him smile and relax. Paloma the ice breaker.

'Yes, she's wonderful,' Jenna agreed genuinely yet envying her friend's ability to act so naturally with Ross, while she was stiff with tension. But Paloma hadn't shared a past with him as she had.

Jenna slumped down into her chair. Ross slumped nowhere. The icy cool was back and he stood stiffly by the fireplace staring down into the flickering flames of an elegant coal-effect gas fire which her mother loathed. The lease on the apartment stated no real fires which was a cause of great angst to Yvonne who had loved the huge fires at Amersham Hall in England.

Jenna realised that her thoughts were wandering aimlessly and she brought them back under control.

'I didn't know you spoke Spanish so well,' she started, filling that awkward silence which had fallen after Paloma's gushy exit.

'I'd imagine there's a lot about me you don't know,' Ross uttered.

'Why you're here might be a good start to getting to know you then,' she suggested frostily. He had given no reason for this visit yet there must be one. He surely wouldn't just didn't drop in on someone he hadn't seen for years!

He lifted his head and looked at her as she sat curled up in the velvet wing chair across from him. 'I came because I was asked,' he told her quietly.

Jenna widened her eyes in surprise. 'I certainly didn't ask for you!' she uttered and because it was a silly assumption that she had, she added quickly, 'And my mother certainly has no reason to ask you here.'

He ignored the retort and went on, sombrely. 'Yvonne asked me to come and if you don't know why then this is indeed a wasted trip. Not that I thought it ever remotely hinted of success when it was put to me.'

'What are you talking about, Ross?' she asked him impatiently. 'You really are so frustrating. When I do manage to get two words out of you they are in a language I don't understand. What are you getting at and why on earth should my mother ask you to come here when she hasn't set eyes on you for three years!'

She noticed the hand on the mantelpiece tighten into a fist and the knuckles whiten with the effort. His piercing blue eyes were relentlessly icy as he turned his head towards her.

'Hasn't it occurred to you that tea is taking rather a

long time? Can't you see the state your mother is in, how anxious she is? She is purposely leaving us alone together in the hope that I can talk some sense into you.'

Jenna stared at him blankly. What an earth was he talking about?

'And don't turn on the wide-eyed innocence, Jenna,' he said harshly. 'It never worked with me and hasn't a chance now. You might as well know from the start that I don't feel the same way as Yvonne. Personally I don't care who you marry but Yvonne asked me to come and –'

Jenna was suddenly on her feet, so swiftly and unexpectedly the action stopped Ross in full flow. Her heart froze with realisation and her words came out hotly.

'My mother asked you to come and stop my wedding!' she exclaimed in shocked exasperation. 'And that is why you are here? But she can't do that! How dare she; how dare you! This is outrageous!'

'I was desperate, Jenna,' her mother spoke softly behind her and Jenna swung around to face her, her heart racing so wildly that she hadn't heard Yvonne come into the room.

'Desperate!' she breathed faintly, her face suddenly flushed with concern.

'I needed a mediator, Jenna,' her mother reasoned calmly. 'I needed someone who knew you and could reason wisely and sensibly and talk you out of making the biggest mistake of your life. Marcel is not right for you and –'

Jenna stared at her mother in confusion. She couldn't believe this. It was impossible. Her whole being revolted against the thought that her mother had even considered such a thing; sending for Ross, Ross of all people, to stop her wedding!

'And you sent for *him*?' she laughed in disbelief, still hardly able to take it on board. Her face suddenly pinched with anguish and her voice dragged up from her throat in a hoarse whisper as she verbally attacked her mother.

'We hate each other, Mamma, we always have done and we always will and you have made the biggest mistake of your life by asking *him* to come here and reason on your behalf. He's just told me he doesn't care a damn who I marry and why should he anyway?'

'Please, Jenna,' Yvonne interjected desperately, 'spend some time with Ross, listen to him and –'

'Listen to *him*!' she cried, her hands clenched in to fists at her side. Wildly she turned her attention to Ross who was standing stiffly, eyes down, obviously hating every second of this row. And Jenna hated *him* for being here, breathing the same air as her, taking up her space, being a part of all this.

'Ross says *nothing*!' she blurted bitterly. 'Ross is saying nothing now, he never has and he never will,' she taunted him. Then she flashed her furious eyes at her mother who was watching her with deep distress clouding hers. 'He doesn't want to be here, Mamma, because he doesn't care and never has done. You have embarrassed him by asking him here, you have embarrassed *me* a thousand-fold and if you think his presence will make any difference to my decision to marry Marcel you are very much mistaken. In fact...' her breath caught in her throat and she had to force the words out because they hurt so much to say. 'In fact it strengthens my determination. I will marry Marcel. I don't care that you are against this marriage. This is my life and I will do with it what I like. Nothing you say or do will stop me. I am going to marry Marcel DeLuc!'

How dare her mother do this to her? How dare Ross respond to Yvonne's bizarre request for help? He didn't care, anyway, whether she lived or died or married the monster from the deep! Ross didn't damn well care!

In a blind, hurting fury she tried to hurl herself around the wing chair to get out of the room, unable to face what her mother had done a second longer. Bringing the one man in the world who reminded her of her embarrassing past with him back into her life. But her toe caught the leg of the chair and she lurched forward. Ross caught her firmly and held her by her upper arms and the effect on her was electric. Her whole body went into shock and the blood drained from her flushed face. Ross was looking down at her with concern; their eyes locked for an instant and then in a fury she managed to find the strength to step away from him. But for the life of her she couldn't break the eye contact between them. It was ecstasy *and* a cruel reminder of just how much he was still in her heart.

Suddenly the salon doors flew open. Completely unaware of the argument and tension in the room, Paloma bounced in clutching Jenna's dress-box.

'Jenna, your wedding dress. Don't say you've forgotten it. It's growing on me now,' she gushed. 'I didn't think it would at first but I guess anything goes these days and Marcel is an artist after all. What do you think, Yvonne?'

Jenna froze. They were like a tableau. Ross, her

mother, herself, all frozen in time. Paloma, all innocence and bubbling with excitement, not knowing the damage she was doing to Jenna's heart-rate, slid off the top of the box. She rustled aside the tissue and held the burgundy silk cocktail dress up for everyone to see.

Jenna watched it all as if in slow motion, the dress sliding out of the box, shimmering down to the floor as Paloma held it up by the shoulders. Through a mist she heard her mother gasp, saw her stiffen and gaze at the dress, eyes wide and distraught at her daughter's inappropriate choice of wedding dress. Piercing through it all came Ross's muttered exclamation, for her ears only. 'Oh, why, Jenna? Why *do* you do the things you do?'

In a whirl of hot embarrassment she was suddenly acutely aware of Ross reaching out for her arm again as if she had tripped once more. But there was a subtle change in his touch. A softening of the grip, softening to a reassuring caress...as if he pitied her for what she had done, bought a *pitifully* unsuitable dress to be married in.

And then Jenna's head started to clear and the realisation of why she had bought the wretched dress suddenly came to her. It was there in front of her; her mother's appalled, deeply shocked expression. She knew then she had bought the dress for just that effect, to urge her mother out of her lethargic indifference to her wedding and to help her.

But what sort of help was she expecting of her mother? Jenna asked herself in confusion. She knew her own mind. She wanted to marry Marcel, didn't she?

Suddenly Yvonne let out a cry of despair and flew

from the room. In dismay Jenna watched her, frustrated that her mother was turning her back on her once again.

But was it because Ross was here? Her mother was against the wedding, otherwise why ask him to come and talk Jenna out of it? But why him and not Alastair? She didn't understand any of it.

She moved then, wrenched her arm from Ross's grip and dashed towards her friend. She took the dress from Paloma and flung it back into the box. 'I...I've changed my mind,' she mumbled. 'You were right, it isn't suitable.'

She bit her lower lip and then swung round to face Ross to find him studying her intently and her mind flashed back to just a short while previously when she had entered the room. As she had stopped in the doorway at the sight of him she had known that it wasn't possible to put the past behind her and forget him. Her heart had jumped sickeningly. It had thudded as it had never thudded for Marcel or any other man.

Now she lifted her chin defiantly because his words were still ringing in her ears. Hurting her and making her want to hurt him back for his coldness. "Personally I don't care who you marry." But whatever she said wouldn't make any difference, not to him.

She was the wild child once again as she blurted out at him. 'It's going to be a white wedding. Lace and satin and flowers and choral singing. Your trip is wasted, Ross. You must be very relieved to hear that your opinion isn't wanted. Nothing will stop me marrying Marcel DeLuc. Not you, or my mother's strange attitude, nothing!'

Clutching the box to her breast she fled from the

room, nearly colliding with Chantelle and the tea trolley. She hurtled up the short flight of steps, along the corridor to her bedroom and slammed the door behind her.

She flung the box onto the bed, pummelled the lid with her fists and fell across it, crying her heart out for the first time in many years.

chapter five

Ross was still awake at three in the morning. Hot and uncomfortable in an unfamiliar bed he kicked off the covers and pulled on his robe. He stood by the long window where an ill-fitting frame allowed a breeze through to cool his brow.

The view of a moon-bathed Seine was beautiful but he couldn't fully appreciate it. He didn't want to be here and yet at the sight of Jenna standing transfixed in the salon doorway earlier he hadn't wanted to be anywhere else in the world.

He damned himself for having felt that way. He damned Jenna for provocatively twirling his pearl against the hollow of her throat. Had she known what she was doing, reminding him of that night? Did she always wear it or was it merely a coincidence that she had been wearing it on this very day? Did he care? He knew the answer to that but it didn't help to know that his heart still ached for her.

He sighed deeply, wide awake, because the night had been fraught and had left its mark: insomnia. Jenna hadn't put in an appearance for tea or dinner later. She had remained closeted in her room, even refusing Paloma's pleas to come out. No one else had dared to approach her, including himself. It had reminded him of days of old. Some things never changed, he thought ruefully.

But it was disturbing to witness Jenna's obvious unhappiness. True she had been furious with her mother for asking him to come to Paris to mediate over her wedding plans and he could well understand her anger, but he felt it went deeper than that.

The wedding dress. Knowing Jenna he wouldn't have been unduly surprised if a frothy bright-red creation had leapt out of that box in the guise of a wedding dress. But the dull, drab, burgundy had shaken him. It would probably have looked stunning on a forty-year-old but would be a shroud on a young, vibrant bride such as Jenna would surely be. And instead of a fiery defiance for her choice of wedding attire, as he had expected, she had been crippled with embarrassment at its exposure to everyone. No, something wasn't right here and it pained him to think that the dress might have been a deep-seated psychological cry for help. But for the life of him he couldn't come up with a reason for why that should be.

He was about to turn away from the window back to his bed to seek some rest before the dawn broke when something across the cobbled boulevard below caught his eye. A small figure leaning over the grey stone parapet alongside the river. He strained his eyes through a faint drizzle. Dear God it was Jenna. Out there on her own, gazing out over the black river, as if...

Hurriedly he dressed and dashed through the apartment, grabbing a coat from the stand in the hall before leaping down the stairs and outside into the Paris drizzle.

Jenna jumped as he draped the coat around her shoulders and protectively drew her hard against his side to warm her.

To his surprise she didn't protest but shivered and snuggled into the comforting fabric.

'I wasn't going to throw myself in,' she told him as she gazed across the water to the riverside lights on the opposite embankment.

'I didn't think for a minute you were,' he told her softly, slightly unnerved that she had said such a thing; very unnerved that it was the same thought that had come to him on sight of her down here on her own. He was right he was sure. Jenna wasn't happy and if all was well with this proposed marriage, shouldn't she be?

'Couldn't you sleep?' he asked.

'Couldn't you?'

He smiled ruefully. 'I'm a creature of habit and prefer my own bed. What's your excuse?'

'Conscience,' she admitted softly. 'I was beastly to everyone tonight, Paloma's last night as well.' She turned her face towards him. It was damp and Ross wanted to smooth his fingers over her creamy skin and feel her warmth. She smiled thinly. 'I was beastly to you too and that wasn't fair. You didn't ask for all this.'

Ross raised his brows in surprise. 'An apology? You *have* changed, Jenna.'

'That wasn't an apology, Ross, and you won't get one either,' she told him calmly. 'I'm still mad with you for coming but madder with my mother for asking you to come. My marriage has nothing to do with anyone but me and Marcel.'

All spoken in a droning monotone that Ross was unfamiliar with. She usually spoke to him in a tone several octaves higher. Screaming pitch actually.

'I agree,' he told her, nodding his head. 'It's your future, not anyone else's.'

'If you thought that, why did you come?' she shrugged.

Ross let her go and leaned on the parapet beside her, clenching his hands together. 'I felt obliged to,' he admitted. 'My father started pulling emotional strings, about your mother being in a state over your forthcoming marriage.'

'If he was so worried about her he should have come himself,' Jenna retorted.

'Your mother wanted me to come,' he explained. 'Perhaps she's not ready to face my father yet and besides, if he had come it might have confused her thinking. She might have put her own feelings before yours. This is all about you after all.'

Jenna sighed and pulled the coat tighter around her. 'So she calls in the troops and you arrive. She can't talk to me about my own wedding, but she can talk to you about it. I'm beginning to wonder about her motives.'

'What do you mean?'

Jenna's eyes widened plaintively. 'She's never even met him, Ross. She doesn't want me to marry him yet she has never met him. She says the gossip is enough for her. He's unsuitable – end of story to her.'

'She has a point. He does have a bit of a reputation.'

'He's changed,' Jenna told him determinedly. 'He wants to settle down as much as I do. His father is ambitious and the last thing Marcel wants to do is taint his father's name with his former wild ways. His father, Gerard, is up for the Presidency, you know,' she added rather flippantly.

Ross smiled to himself. 'And marriage to you would help, would it?'

'I didn't mean that, Ross. I'm just trying to stress the fact that Marcel isn't the rebel he used to be. He has family commitments and duties now.'

Ross sighed deeply. 'Have you told your mother all this?'

'She won't listen,' Jenna groaned. 'She just doesn't want to talk about it.'

'And yet she has called on me to talk for her,' Ross mused. 'I'm inclined to agree with you. Yvonne is acting rather strangely.'

Jenna laughed lightly. 'Wow, we agree on something at last, my mother's peculiar attitude.' She shrugged into her coat. 'It changes nothing though. I would have liked her support but I shall marry Marcel all the same, with or without her approval. Your journey is wasted, Ross. You can go back to your father and report that you have failed to change my mind. I'd imagine that won't come too easily to you. You don't like failure, do you?'

Ross narrowed his eyes at her, wondering exactly what she meant by that. But he didn't ask because his feelings weren't the issue here.

'I'm not familiar with failure, Jenna,' he told her coolly, 'so I can't say how I might feel if faced with it. I stress the word if. I haven't failed, yet.'

Jenna glanced at him warily. 'What do you mean?'

Ross inclined his head towards her to stress his point.

'I'm not leaving Paris till I get to the bottom of all this,' he told her softly but determinedly

Jenna's eyes widened. 'To the bottom of what?' she blurted.

'I'm getting bad vibes about this forthcoming wedding.'

'Your presence is causing them, Ross. Everything was just fine till you turned up. I resent you interfering when it's nothing to do with you.'

'Everything wasn't *just fine* before I arrived, Jenna. How can it be when your mother is so adamantly opposed to it? You are barely speaking to her. And as for that wedding dress...' He sighed deeply. 'That was no mistake, Jenna. You purposely bought it to cause a furore.'

'I did not!'

Ross smiled thinly. 'You know, I'm not an expert on the workings of a woman's mind...'

'Huh, you can say that again!' Jenna interrupted huffily, glaring hard across the river.

'But I reckon that a woman in *love*,' he went on, putting stress on the word love, 'would want to look her very best on the most important day of her life. The dress you bought was totally out of character for you. I know you said you had changed your mind about it but frankly, I didn't believe a word of it'

She turned to him then, her eyes narrowed warily. 'Just what are you getting at?' she seethed.

'The point of me staying on in Paris,' he told her calmly, holding her eyes. 'I'm curious, you see, Jenna; curious to know why you are considering marrying a man you don't love.'

As Jenna's mouth dropped open Ross knew he had struck home with that rather cruel observation. It gave him no satisfaction to see her lips suddenly tighten determinedly, as if it was beneath her to deny that he was wrong. Ross concentrated on her eyes and was dismayed to see tears fill them. The hurt he had inflicted on her pained him greatly but he knew he had to pursue it, for her own sake.

'Why, Jenna, why marry a man you don't love? To spite your mother?' Ross persisted.

There was no reply from Jenna, not a word. So he was right. If he was wrong she would vehemently deny his suggestion, surely?

'And while we are on the subject of love,' he ground out. 'Is this man more interested in his father's career than you, because that is the way it is coming across to me? You have given no indication that this proposed marriage is based on love.'

He watched as she ran the tip of her tongue over her dry lips. At last she spoke in a thin voice.

'You wouldn't recognise love, Ross. You haven't the vision. Just like your father, you are too hard, too immersed in your work to notice anything remotely human going on around you. I'm not a corporate body to be dealt with in the boardroom of your mind. I would have more respect for your opinions and observations if they came from the heart and not from what is expected of you. You're little more than a robot, working to your father's will.'

She started to turn away from him but Ross caught her arm and spun her back to face him. He held her very firmly by her shoulders.

'So you think a handful of insults will send me on my way with my tail between my legs?' he accused her. 'Wrong, Jenna. I'm not that easily put off.'

'But you were once!' she suddenly insisted angrily. 'Let me remind you in case you have forgotten. Years ago you let me walk away from you,' she dragged herself out of his grasp, lifted a hand and clicked her fingers, 'just like that! So what is stopping you from walking away from me this time?'

Ross froze. It was the very first reference to their past. The reminder sliced through him like an ice-pick. Had it troubled her as much as it had troubled him over the years? Though they had met on a few bruising occasions after that night and before Yvonne defected back to Paris, neither of them had ever spoken of it. They had avoided each other rather than face it. Now was different. She was on the brink of marriage and circumstances had forced them together again.

'Well it damn well isn't going to happen again,' he told her stoically. He grasped her again: a firm grip she was powerless to shrug off this time. 'I'm not letting you go through with a loveless wedding ceremony, Jenna, until you convince me that you are doing the right thing and then...only then...' His voice failed him.

Could he do it? Allow her to walk out of his life yet again? He glared down at her, searching her lovely, troubled features for something that would give him the courage to admit that the last thing he wanted was to see her married to another man. But the truth was that he would have to let her go if she was truly in love and Marcel returned her feelings. The bottom line was that if she was happy, really happy, he would have to accept it and get on with his own life.

She lifted her chin proudly. 'I don't have to give you any explanations for my actions, Ross.'

'But you do, Jenna,' he insisted. 'Because we all care about you. Me, your mother and Alastair. Especially me...' he hesitated slightly. 'You mentioned the past and...'

'And it's still on your conscience,' she finished for him with contempt, her eyes flashing wildly at him. 'Perhaps that is what this is really about,' she went on bitingly. 'You came here to spoil it all for me because you know something about me my fiancé doesn't! That I will be a great disappointment on my wedding night because I'm not the virgin he expects me to be. You were there before him! Is that your wicked revenge on me? To remind me of something I've been trying to forget for years?'

Ross gazed at her in utter astonishment. He stood as though frozen in time, unable to move for the pain that flooded his body. Her impassioned words spun in his head. How deeply he must have hurt her that night, in body and spirit. Her shame must be profound: equal to his. And the implication that she was not already sleeping with her fiancé shocked him deeply. She had admitted that Marcel expected her to be a virgin on their wedding night.

Had there been anyone in her life since her eighteenth birthday? Had he done that to her? Put her off men until now? The thought was appalling.

'Never, Jenna, never did I think anything of the sort,' he murmured thickly.

Jenna lowered her head and shook it pitifully. 'I'm sorry,' she whispered. 'I shouldn't have said that. I do and say crazy things at times.' Slowly she lifted her face and met his eyes. 'Go back to England, Ross,' she implored heavily. 'I don't need this complication in my life. Not now. I'm going to marry Marcel. It's going to happen and there is nothing you or anyone else can do about it. Just go home.'

Ross shook his head. 'I can't do that, Jenna.'

She steeled herself in his grip. 'Why – because of duty to your father and my mother?'

He stared bleakly at her, his thoughts perilous. This was nothing to do with duty. The night of her birthday was a power to be reckoned with. It had got him here to Paris and it was going to keep him here because even now he felt her magnetism. Pale and tired and crumpled into her coat she looked so delicately vulnerable he just wanted to pull her against him and hold her forever.

When she lifted her face to look into his eyes all those old feelings surged through his body. The need to totally possess her in every way. But she wasn't eighteen anymore and was promised to another man. Yet knowing that he was helpless to stop himself.

He lowered his head. Jenna moaned softly as his mouth closed over hers. A heart-rending moan of despair. Her soft, warm, silky lips under his made his head spin and was a bitter sweet reminder of the most passionate night of his life: never to be equalled, never to be surpassed. The kiss deepened as he crushed her mouth so ardently she responded by parting her lips and clinging to him fiercely. And then her whole body trembled and he realised she was crying.

He drew his mouth back from hers and buried his face in her hair. His heart was thundering with feeling for her. 'I'm not turning my back on you, Jenna,' he said fiercely, kissing her ear. 'Convince me you are doing the right thing and I'll leave you alone.'

Suddenly she let out a heart wrenching sob of anguish and fiercely tore herself away from him. Her eyes were glazed, wild, angry as she glared up at him.

'I'll give you what you want, Ross; the truth from my heart,' she sobbed. 'I...I love Marcel with a passion I have never felt before in my whole miserable little life. Marcel worships the ground I walk on. It's why we are going to be married. To be together because that is what true love is all about. Nothing you say or do will stop us. Get out of my life, Ross. Do the honourable thing and get out of my life, now!'

With that she turned and flew across the deserted boulevard to the apartment block. Ross stood like stone and watched her furiously bang the entrance door behind her.

He stood for a very long time staring out over the oily water till the pale dawn turned it to silver. He was cold and damp but his mouth still burned with the touch of her lips. Had she responded to his impulsive kiss? So dazed himself he wasn't sure how she had taken it. She had clung to him though. He could still feel her fingertips clawing into his back.

For years she had been a desperate ache in his heart. And now? His hand moved slowly to his chest. Now he hurt like hell: more than ever. He was his own worst enemy, coming here and putting himself through more angst. He didn't need these emotions in his life, but the worst realisation of all was that he now knew he would never get over her. Finally she had given him what he wanted – his freedom – but it wasn't a release. She loved Marcel. He hadn't wanted to hear it and that was going to be a life sentence for him to live with. Purgatory.

"I'll give you what you want, Ross," she had said before heatedly admitting her love for her fiancé.

Ross plunged his hands into his pockets and, head bowed, he started to walk along the embankment. Was it possible she had lied just to be rid of him? Was his presence troubling her because of their past? Was he an unwelcome embarrassment to her in the run-up to her wedding?

He didn't know. Perhaps he would never know. Jenna claimed to be speaking from her heart but how could he ever be sure with her? She had lied before, claiming she had had lovers when he knew he had been her first. Lies were often her defence mechanism.

Ross stopped and turned back towards the apartment. It was because of that uncertainty that he knew he would stay in Paris for however long it took to find out the truth. At whatever cost to his own heart, he was staying because what she had just admitted wasn't ringing true with him.

Jenna in love and happily looking forward to her wedding day, in spite of her mothers disapproval, hadn't driven her to buy a ridiculous wedding gown, hadn't driven her to lock herself in her bedroom all night, or to emerge in the early hours of the morning to shiver on a cold wet boulevard overlooking an inhospitable river.

Jenna was in emotional hell for some reason and Ross needed to know why.

chapter six

'Jenna left a message for you,' Yvonne said anxiously as Ross stepped into the kitchen the next morning.

He glanced at his watch. It was gone eleven. He'd snatched a few hours of troubled sleep but felt no better for it. It had been daylight when he had finally got to bed and that wasn't normally his routine. He felt ragged, drained of all feeling because for once in his life he couldn't come to a rational decision. Should he step back and let Jenna have her way, happy or unhappy in her decision to marry? Last night he had been determined to stay and get to the truth of the matter. Now...now damn it, he wasn't sure.

'A message, eh? Where is she?' He reached for the coffee pot as he sat down at a small round table across from Yvonne. Glancing at the headlines of *Le Nouvel Observateur* he slid the paper aside with disinterest to pour himself a coffee.

'She's taken Paloma to the airport,' Yvonne said hurriedly as she got up to fuss with a pan on the cooker. 'I'll make you some breakfast. It's Chantelle's day off. Jenna said to say goodbye and to give Alastair her very best wishes.' The pan clattered on the hob and Ross turned to look at her. Yvonne looked as if she was about to burst into tears.

'She...she said you would be leaving today. Please, Ross, please don't go. I can't stop Jenna's wedding without your help. You must stay. You must!'

Ross ran an unsteady hand through his hair. 'Yvonne, sit down and calm down. I don't want any breakfast, thank you and I haven't made any plans to return to England yet.'

Yvonne sighed with relief and slumped down in a chair. Ross watched her with curiosity as she poured a coffee for herself. Her long delicate fingers were trembling as she spooned sugar into her cup.

Ross wondered at her state of mind. Though elegantly dressed in a pale blue silk shirt and pale linen pants, her make-up as perfect as usual, her dark hair coiled at the nape of her neck, he guessed her appearance belied the way she was feeling.

Yesterday when he had arrived he had been shocked by her nervous tension. Because of Paloma's presence last night at tea and dinner nothing had been said about her concerns for Jenna's engagement. He supposed he was in for it now.

'How is Alastair, Ross?' Yvonne asked plaintively. 'I know we speak on the phone, but I never really know how he is.'

The question took him aback momentarily. He had expected her to launch into Jenna's wedding plans as that was the point of her asking him to stay.

'He misses you. He won't admit it of course, he's too proud and stubborn, but he misses you,' Ross told her truthfully. 'I can't get him to retire properly yet. He still gets involved with the company but I suspect his heart's not in it. Anyway I'm not here to pass judgement on you two. You're old enough to make your own mistakes. Is that why you wanted me here and not Alastair? His presence might complicate things?'

'Something like that,' Yvonne said quietly, studying her coffee cup and not looking at him. 'Jenna mustn't go through with this wedding,' she said adamantly. 'It isn't right for her. I want her happiness and I don't want her to make the same mistakes I've made in my life.'

Ross understood her reasoning but without talking it over with her daughter how was she so certain Jenna was going to make a mistake?

'I'm sure every parent wants the best for their children, Yvonne, but she's a big girl now and old enough to make her own decisions.'

Yvonne's head shot up in alarm. 'I asked you here for help, Ross, and I don't want to hear you siding with her. I want you to talk her out of it, not go along with her. She'll listen to you. She's always hung on every word you have ever spoken...'

'Don't be absurd, Yvonne,' Ross laughed cynically. 'She can't stand the sight of me. She's rebelled against everything I've ever said and always will.'

'You're wrong. Jenna adores you. You can influence her when no one else can get through to her. Talk to her, spend some time together. Make her realise that what she is doing isn't right for her!'

Ross sighed heavily and poured more coffee. Yvonne's desperation was really coming over now. She must be hallucinating if she thought Jenna had ever adored him and he was in with a chance of stopping this marriage.

What the hell was he doing here? The cold light of day was getting to him. He was reasoning sensibly when he hadn't before. Last night's decision to get to the root of Jenna's emotions was waning now. Jenna was determined to marry and a determined Jenna was a power not even the devil himself could oppose.

'I've already talked to her,' he said on a sigh. 'Our paths crossed in the early hours of the morning. She's upset by your attitude, Yvonne. You should be talking to her about her wedding, not me! She needs your support.'

Ross stood up. He'd had enough. He had his own demons to contend with without Yvonne's near-hysterics.

'Where are you going?' she whispered fearfully.

'To use the phone if I may,' he told her shortly. 'I have a business associate here in Paris I'd like to meet up with before I leave. Hopefully I can fix an appointment...' He didn't finish.

Yvonne shot to her feet and grabbed at the edge of the table to steady herself.

'Damn you, Ross!' she cried hysterically. 'You are the mirror image of your damned father, a blasted carbon copy. Always business. I thought you had a heart where Jenna is concerned but you don't give a damn, just like your father with me. How can you do this, just walk away?'

Ross raked his hand through his hair in frustration, refusing to rise to her insults. 'Yvonne, Jenna loves the guy,' he reasoned calmly. 'There is nothing any of us can do to dissuade her. They are going to be married and...'

'They are *not* going to be married!' Yvonne stated fiercely. 'And she can't love him, Ross!' she implored, suddenly deathly pale and shaking from head to toe. 'She can't love him and he can't love her. They are not *allowed* to love.'

Ross frowned with concern. 'I don't understand you, Yvonne. You are beginning to sound obsessive over this. Why can't you accept what is about to happen?'

'Be..because...' In anguish she pressed her fingers to her temples as if trying to clear her head. And then she lifted her face and looked at him, tears streaming down her face. 'The marriage is impossible, Ross,' she whispered hoarsely. 'It must *never* happen, never!' She paused to draw a long agonised breath. 'Gerard...Gerard DeLuc is...is Jenna's father! Don't you see? Don't you understand? They have the same father. M..Marcel is her half brother!'

Ross felt as if he had been shot. He recoiled back from the table, the pain real, low in his stomach, like a bullet wound, hot, searing and sharp. The coffee he had just drank rose bitterly to the back of his throat. He felt every last drop of his blood drain out of him.

In mute disbelief he stared at Yvonne wondering if he had heard right, but the intensity of the echo in his head was for real. *Jenna and Marcel shared the same father.* Absurdly he imagined Yvonne was so determined to stop the wedding she was inventing this ghastly, dreadful, wicked lie to get her own way. But surely no mother could be so cruel?

Suddenly he was forced to move swiftly. He caught Yvonne before she collapsed to the floor, sobbing hysterically.

Gently Ross eased her on to a chair. Before his brain fully kicked in he walked out of the kitchen to the salon where he found a bottle of brandy. He moved like the robot Jenna accused him of being, not feeling, his mind a shocked blank. Back in the kitchen he poured two glasses, his hand rock steady but sweat suddenly breaking out on his brow. He'd just been delivered into a living nightmare which didn't bear thinking about.

'Drink this,' he said softly to Yvonne, taking her shaking hand from the top of the table and guiding it towards the glass. She grasped it and lifted it to her trembling lips. Ross sat down heavily, lifted his own glass and swallowed hard. It worked quickly; steadying his pulse rate, clearing his head. His first emotion was anger at Yvonne for holding this terrible secret deep inside her for so long but compassion followed quickly. For a mother to have to bear this was unthinkable.

Yvonne was crying quietly now as she reached out for Ross's hand and clutched at it desperately.

'H...how could I tell her, Ross,' she wept, her head lowered shamefully. 'When she was small she used to ask about her real father but I always side-stepped the issue. When she became a teenager she stopped asking. If only I'd had the strength to tell her when she was a child.' She lifted her pinched face. 'I was ashamed you see, so deeply ashamed of bearing an illegitimate child. I was a student at the time and...and naive...I didn't know he was already married with a baby...'

'It's all right, Yvonne,' Ross soothed, his throat dry with emotion. 'You don't have to explain to me.'

He sighed deeply and despondently. But there was some explaining to do to Jenna. The weight of his heart was leaden inside him. The shock would tip her over the edge of sanity. All her young life had been troubled and now, just when she thought she had found happiness...to have it shattered so cruelly.

'But you will have to explain to Jenna,' Ross reasoned softly but urgently. 'She has to know, before this goes any further. You must tell her. Now. Today.'

Yvonne's misty eyes widened in terror. 'I can't, Ross. I can't do that. It's why I asked you to come. Alastair doesn't know. It would have shamed me to tell him about my past. I've always led him to believe I was married to Jenna's father. You must think of another way to stop this wedding. Jenna must never know. No one must ever know my terrible secret. You *must* do this for me, Ross,' she pleaded urgently.

Ross's blood turned to ice. Slowly he withdrew his hand from Yvonne's. He suddenly saw everything in a new light and didn't like it one bit. Yvonne was using him in the cruellest way, expecting him to contrive to stop Jenna marrying her half brother and to keep it all quiet. It was impossible. Dishonest. Suddenly he was even more angry with Yvonne for her selfishness and for landing him with this serious problem. But he suppressed his anger to speak calmly.

'I won't do that, Yvonne. Jenna must know the truth however painful for everyone. It is your duty as a caring mother to tell her everything, everything you have told me.'

'I can't! I won't! You forced the truth out of me,' she cried unreasonably. 'I just wanted you to talk her out of the wedding without knowing the truth, but you gave me no choice but to tell you. You have been siding with her, wanting this marriage for her, so you forced me to tell you. You must shoulder some of the blame and help me out!'

Ross could scarcely believe the injustice of this accusation. Yvonne's selfishness and cowardice disgusted him. Couldn't she see that she owed her daughter the truth? A small part of him wanted to get up and go and leave this sorry mess behind him but he knew that was impossible. As impossible as talking Jenna out of this marriage without the truth.

Could he summon the strength to tell Jenna everything if Yvonne was adamant that *she* wouldn't? Was there any way out of this without deep, deep pain all round?

He spoke at last, honestly, because it was the only way: straight to the jugular.

'Yvonne, you must be strong about this. You have to face the fact that this was your mistake many years ago and no fault of Jenna's. You should have nipped this relationship in the bud from the start. They are in a relationship that is taboo. You knew that from the beginning and you shouldn't have let it go on...'

'I tried to stop it,' Yvonne protested. 'But you know Jenna. She's wilful.'

'But didn't it cross your mind that...' The thought sickened him and the words wouldn't come but he had to force them on Yvonne because he had to stress the seriousness of what she had done to her daughter. 'Think about it, Yvonne,' he went on gravely, 'Jenna is already engaged to the man. They are in a relationship and...'

After their talk earlier he knew that Jenna wasn't

intimate with Marcel in the sexual sense but it must have crossed Yvonne's mind. How could she have allowed her pride and selfishness to let that slide by?

'My daughter is pure, Ross, if that is what you are getting at,' Yvonne said indignantly. 'A mother knows these things. Jenna has never been with a man, ever. I've always taught her moral values and I'd stake my life on her purity in that sense.' She drew breath. 'Jenna has her faults but promiscuity isn't one of them.'

Ross lowered his eyes and frowned. No point in pursuing that line of persuasion. Only he and Jenna knew otherwise. But where to go from here? The wedding had to be stopped. It was imperative now. But how?

'How on earth do you expect me to talk Jenna out of marriage without the truth, Yvonne?' Ross asked. 'It will be impossible. The more you show opposition the more determined she will become.' He shook his head, adamant that he was right. 'She has to know the truth. It's the only way to stop it.'

Yvonne shook her head and lifted the brandy glass to her lips again. When she finally met his eyes she murmured plaintively. 'I haven't the strength to tell her, Ross. I can't begin to form the words. I know what you are saying is right but I can't do it myself. If it has to come out it...it will have to come from you. I can't face the shame of telling her myself.'

He had half expected that. To have Yvonne's emotional burden firmly placed on his shoulders. He wondered how she had ever had the guts to walk out on his father. But if she hadn't they wouldn't all be in this mess now. Another *if* that didn't warrant further thought.

'You are being totally unreasonable, Yvonne,' Ross protested gravely.

'What about?' Jenna asked from the doorway.

Ross and Yvonne jumped. Ross's heart seemed to cave in. How long had she been in the apartment? Had she heard more than his last words? He watched her through new eyes as she stepped into the kitchen and reached for the brandy bottle on the table. He saw her beauty, her slight but perfect figure in designer jeans and a baggy grey sweatshirt. He saw her total innocence in all this and he saw her future where nothing would be the same for her again.

In that moment he wanted to lift her, bury his face in her scented hair and carry her away from all this. To escape with her where no one could touch them, to love and nurture her and care for her as no one had ever done before.

'Brandy to toast my future?' she said lightly as she studied the label. 'Well it'll be champagne tomorrow. I called Marcel from the airport and he'll be back from Spain in the morning.' She directed her gaze at her mother. 'I've invited him for dinner so you can meet him at last, Mamma.' She fluttered her jet lashes in Ross's direction. 'Shame you won't be here, Ross.'

Ross was sharply aware of the grating of Yvonne's chair on the tiled floor and her swift exit from the room. He heard her hurried steps across the hallway and up the short flight of steps and her bedroom door shutting behind her.

But there was no easy escape for him. He was

shocked by the knowledge he held; delivered so unexpectedly by Yvonne. He sat stiffly at the table and in silence watched Jenna fill the kettle. He heard the phone persistently ringing in the hallway but it wasn't answered. Time stood still. The walls seemed to close in around him.

He knew the truth about Jenna's parentage – something she didn't know – and the knowledge was crippling him. He didn't want this terrible burden he was carrying for her but the thought of sharing it with her was so much worse. But would she believe him if he blurted it out to her now?

'So you see what I'm up against, Ross,' she sighed. 'She can't bear to be in the same room as me. What was she being unreasonable about then? Don't tell me. I know. You and Mamma have obviously been discussing my wedding and you have clearly not convinced her I'm doing the right thing. I'd say you have failed twice over.' She shrugged her narrow shoulders dismissively. 'Once she meets Marcel she'll change her mind. Tough if she doesn't! More coffee before you leave?'

Ross wasn't going anywhere, of that he was certain. He hadn't the heart to turn his back on her as easily as her mother was capable of doing. All the same he wished for a thunderbolt: an earthquake, a catastrophe, any disaster to get him out of what he had to do.

'I'm not going anywhere, Jenna,' he said soberly. He cleared his throat. Sooner rather than later he was going to tell her. Marcel's presence was imminent, the following morning in fact. This all had to be sorted before then. The phone started ringing again, grating against his raw nerve endings. 'Doesn't anyone answer a phone in this house!' he snapped.

'I'll get it,' Jenna laughed. 'Your nerves are bad this morning. Serves you right for staying up all night, old man.'

Ross held his head in his hands, wondering if that would be the last time he'd ever hear her laugh. As soon as she came back he was going to tell her just why she couldn't marry Marcel. There was no choice. It had to be done. Through a tunnel he heard Jenna's frantic cry for him. 'Ross! Ross! Come quickly.'

Ross flew into the hallway. Tears were streaming down Jenna's face as she thrust the phone at him. 'It's...it's Charlotte, your Dad's housekeeper...your father's collapsed. He's had a heart attack!'

Blindly Ross snatched the phone from her hand. Jenna stepped back, ringing her hands with anguish.

'It happened this morning, Mr Cameron. He came down for breakfast but refused it. Later I made him a cup of tea and took it through to his study and he just collapsed over his desk. I called the ambulance and the paramedics took him to the hospital.'

'How bad is it?' Ross managed to breathe. He felt as if his chest was crashing inwards.

'They won't say but you'd better come home, Mr Cameron. He was asking for you when they took him away.'

'I'm on my way, Charlotte. Let the hospital know I'm leaving Paris immediately.'

'I'm coming with you, Ross,' Jenna said determinedly, wiping away her tears as Ross shakily put down the phone.

The truth hit him then, sharply. Only minutes ago he had wished for a catastrophe to help him out of the mess he was in. Well it had been delivered with a vengeance. His beloved father's collapse. He'd never forgive himself if his father didn't pull through this and he'd never forgive Yvonne for summoning him to Paris when he should have been with his father.

'Ross, I said I'm coming with you,' Jenna whispered at his side.

He looked down at her and, through his shock at the terrible news he had just received, he was able to reason that this was an appalling blessing in disguise. With Jenna at his side she would be away from Paris and out of Marcel's way. His father's collapse had bought him time, but it was little consolation.

'I'd like that, Jenna,' he said gruffly.

She touched his hand and smiled reassuringly and he thought he saw relief in her eyes, but his heart and head were in such a turmoil he could have been mistaken.

'I'll call a cab and get some flights sorted. I'd better tell, Mamma. She'll want to come too...'

'Jenna, no!'

Ross's head was suddenly spinning. He didn't want that. Yvonne was in no fit state herself to sit at anyone's bedside. On top of everything else she'd be a constant reminder of what he had to do for Jenna. But if his father was gravely ill...

'Mamma still loves him, Ross,' Jenna whispered, looking hurt at Ross's sharp refusal. 'She'd be devastated if...if anything happened to him. We must take her with us. It's only right.'

Ross nodded. *She* was right of course but he didn't dwell on Jenna's concern and depth of feeling for a mother who was letting her daughter down so badly. He only had thoughts for his father's well-being and the need to get to his side as soon as possible.

chapter seven

'The swing is still there,' Jenna murmured as Ross's limousine cruised slowly over the gravel driveway of Amersham Hall, past the pristine lawns and the gnarled old oak tree where the swing hung: unused for years, forlorn and abandoned.

Ross didn't say anything and Jenna wondered at her own crassness in mentioning the swing. As if anything mattered after what Ross had been through this awful day. She glanced at him, wanting to reach out and squeeze his hand but holding back in case a show of caring would be too much for him to bear.

He was more exhausted than anyone. He sat back in his seat with his eyes closed. Anthony, the chauffeur, had been waiting at the airport and had driven them straight to the hospital. Ross had rushed to his father's bedside while she and her mother had worriedly paced the waiting room.

Yvonne had burst into tears when Ross later reported that the heart specialist had said Alastair was a very lucky man. The heart attack was not as bad as was initially thought, but nevertheless was a warning to ease up. He was sedated and resting and was going to make a good recovery. Jenna had watched Ross's face as he had told them the news. In his pale, anguished features she could see how much his father meant to him and how relieved he was.

Jenna sighed as the mansion came into view. She remembered her first sight of it so long ago. Weathered and mellow with a lifetime of variegated ivy clinging to the soft-beige stonework, sunlight glancing off the diamond-paned windows; it had offered so much and yet delivered so little in the end.

'What are you thinking?' Ross asked, as he blinked open his eyes.

'I was just remembering when I first came here,' she murmured. 'Not wanting to be here because I knew it wouldn't last and yet contrarily wanting it to last for ever.'

Ross smiled ruefully. 'I'm not sure I understand that.'

Jenna smiled with him. 'You wouldn't because your life has always been secure. This the only home you've ever known. Before my mother married Alastair, I'd lived all over the place, here, there and everywhere.'

'Yet you rebelled against being here so furiously.'

She shrugged. 'Fear of the unknown I suppose. I didn't know Alastair very well and Mamma's last husband had been so ghastly. Besides I was a terrible teenager. I hated everyone and everything.' She sighed again. 'I wish I was back here under different circumstances though. Your father looked so pale, Ross. Are you sure he's going to be all right?'

'With your mother at his bedside I'm sure he'll be back on his feet in no time,' Ross said tightly.

Jenna nodded as she got out of the car. Ross hadn't looked too pleased at her mother's insistence on staying at the hospital with his father but he had accepted it. She supposed he thought it inappropriate as Yvonne had walked out on Alistair three years before.

'Jenna, how lovely to see you,' the housekeeper enthused as Jenna and Ross stepped into the great hall.

Jenna leaned forward and gave her a hug. 'You are funny, Charlotte. It isn't lovely to see me at all. The last time I saw you I called you all manner of names for losing the bottom half of my bikini in the laundry.'

'Ah, but you apologised when you found it under your bed,' Charlotte laughed.

'Did I? You've a better memory than me then.'

Ross cleared his throat.

'Oh, I'm sorry, Mr Cameron,' Charlotte chuckled. 'Everything is ready as you instructed and thank you for calling me from the hospital to say your father is making a good recovery. I appreciate it as I was so concerned. Now I don't know if I've done right here or not, but Karen called earlier to find out when you were returning from Paris. I had to tell her about your father of course and she was most concerned. I told her you were already on your way home. She said she'll call in later as she would be passing. I didn't get the chance to tell her you were bringing guests home with you. There's plenty of food, so she's welcome to stay for supper...'

'Yes, that's perfectly all right, Charlotte,' Ross said hurriedly.

Jenna stood transfixed, her heart pounding. Ross had a woman in his life. It was odd but she had never considered the possibility. She's been so wrapped up in herself lately that she hadn't thought to ask what he was doing with his life these days. Not that he'd ever done much with it before, apart from business. In all the time she had lived at the Hall, Ross had never brought a woman home. But then she hadn't been back here for three years.

'I...I'd better go up and unpack,' she said quickly. 'Er...same room, Charlotte?'

'Of course, dear.' She reached down for Jenna's bag. 'I'll take you up.'

Without looking at Ross Jenna followed the ample housekeeper up the curving stairway, her heart racing wildly. Karen. The woman in Ross's life. She bit hard on her bottom lip as Charlotte swung open her old bedroom door.

'It's exactly as I remember it,' Jenna breathed, stepping into the lovely room and throwing her shoulder bag down on the lacy bedspread.

'Yes, well nothing much changes around here,' the housekeeper laughed. 'Now tell me, will your mother be coming back tonight as I need to set up in the dining room? Will it be four or just the three of you for supper?'

'Three, Charlotte,' Ross said from the doorway. 'Mrs Cameron has insisted on staying at my father's bedside and won't be coming back tonight and Karen has just called to say she is twenty minutes away.'

'Three it is then,' Charlotte said as she swept out of the room.

'Two,' Jenna told Ross after she had gone. 'I'm tired and need to catch up on some sleep.' She reached for her holdall, lifted it onto the bed and unzipped it without catching Ross's eyes. After all they had been through this day she wasn't ready for meeting Ross's mistress, lover or whatever!

'Do you ever take a meal with anyone?' Ross drawled.

Jenna looked at him then. Leaning in the doorway he appeared lazily elegant in spite of the horrendous day he'd been through.

'Meaning what?'

'Last night in Paris you locked yourself away in your room and tonight you are pulling the same trick. Do you suffer from an embarrassing clicking of your jaw when you eat in front of anyone?'

There was a glimmer of humour in his blue eyes which surprised her.

'As you well know I don't suffer from any such affliction,' she countered, bouncing her silk underwear on to the bedcover.

'Well show some respect for my hospitality and join Karen and me for supper.'

Jenna gritted her teeth. Was he doing this on purpose? Throwing his girlfriend at her to show that he had a life when she had always accused him of not having one?

'Your father is going to be OK and it's obvious your powers of recovery are remarkable but mine aren't, Ross,' she told him stiffly. 'I was terrified for your father, anguished for my mother and my heart was torn out for you today. If you think I can sit down and have a friendly supper with you and your girlfriend then you overestimate my endurance. I'm really, really tired, Ross,' she persisted, pulling a handful of cashmere sweaters from the bottom of her bag.

'And so am I, Jenna,' he said wearily. 'Utterly exhausted. This has been the worst day of my life but I'm not too tired to wonder why you are here.'

She looked at him in alarm. 'What are you hinting at?'

'Back in Paris I was touched that you wanted to support me in my hour of need. I'm now beginning to think you simply wanted to escape for a while.'

Jenna's mouth gaped open and then quickly shut again. She shook her head. 'You mystify me, Ross. I *am* here to support you. Marcel was coming home tomorrow but I was more concerned for you and your father. Why on earth would I want to escape?'

'Because things were getting very stressful for you in Paris.'

'Yes, *you* were making it stressful for me,' she agreed. 'Accusing me of not loving the man I'm going to marry. Making my mother far more hysterical than she was before you arrived. Heavens, if I'd wanted escape I wouldn't have come here with the pair of you. I'd have flown off to Timbuktu, wherever that is!'

'I've misjudged you then,' he admitted with a shrug of his broad shoulders. 'But it doesn't change the fact that I insist on you dining with us. This is my home and my hospitality you are trying to refuse...'

Jenna held up a hand to silence him. 'All right, all right. Have it your own way. I'll dine with you and Karen Dreamboat.' She narrowed her eyes at him. 'At least it will give me a chance to scrutinise her thoroughly and if, just if, you get around to proposing marriage to her, it will give me great pleasure to turn the tables on you and wreck your wedding plans just as you are trying to wreck mine!'

He smiled at her thinly before lifting himself away from the door jamb. 'Little chance of that, Jenna. There isn't a woman born who will ever get me up the aisle.'

Jenna's heart leapt and sank just as quickly. She sat on the edge of the bed after he had gone and held her aching head in her hands. No, Ross wasn't the marrying sort. He hadn't the depth of emotion for such a commitment. It was small consolation that Karen wasn't in there with a chance because neither was she. He was as cynical about marriage as she was. But she was burying that cynicism and moving forward with her life, whereas Ross seemed to be trapped in a time warp.

Charlotte was right, nothing changed around here.

Later, dressed in a simple black cashmere sweater and loose fitting black silk pants Jenna went downstairs. She heard no voices so supposed Karen hadn't arrived yet. She wandered through the open double doors of the drawing room and stood there, hugging herself; surveying the peaceful peach-white and pale-green room overlooking the rose garden. It was dark outside but the room glowed warmly with table lamps.

Ross was standing by the fireplace, hands plunged into the pockets of narrow black trousers, staring into the flames of a huge log fire. His hair was still damp behind his ears after a shower and his shoulders looked tense under a grey fine wool roll-necked sweater. He seemed unaware of her presence so she was able to observe him without him knowing. She imagined his thoughts were with his father but *her* thoughts were reluctantly and guiltily elsewhere. It was here that it had happened, in this very room and though she had been in this room many times since, it had never been at the same time as Ross.

He had loved her so completely here, quickly and

passionately, a tumble of emotions racing through them both and then...then nothing, as if it had never happened.

'Any news from the hospital?' she asked softy as she stepped further into the room.

He looked up and smiled. 'Yvonne just rang. Dad's sleeping peacefully so she's retiring herself. She'll call first thing in the morning. Would you like a glass of wine before supper?'

'Yes, that would be nice. Is Karen here yet?'

He moved towards a side table where a bottle of white wine was cooling in an ice bucket and nodded to the French doors.

Jenna saw the lights of a car moving quickly up the driveway. She steeled herself, but at the same time wondered why she felt the need to brace herself for meeting the woman in Ross's life.

Minutes later she knew the reason why as the tall, elegant, titian-haired beauty flew into the room, flung herself into Ross's arms and clung to him intimately.

Jenna recognised the clench of jealousy in the pit of her stomach. Her heart reeled as Ross stood with his arms around the woman as intimately as Karen was clinging to him. It was as if she didn't exist in this room. This room, hers and Ross's special space...

Clenching her fists tightly she reasoned that she had no right to feel this way. Ross wasn't hers, never had been and never would be. Paris had been bad enough – him on her territory – but she on his? She decided she didn't like Karen, as for Ross...

'I've been so desperately worried for Alastair, Ross,' Karen gushed, stepping back from him and stroking the side of his face. 'Are you sure he's going to be all right?'

'He's having the best possible care and his consultant is confident of a quick recovery,' Ross reassured her. 'I'd like you to meet Jenna.' He nodded his head towards her and as Karen swung around in surprise Jenna felt twelve years old under her sudden icy scrutiny.

Though wearing high heels she felt minuscule against the other woman's towering elegance. Bravely she lifted her chin and extended a hand towards the woman.

'Jenna, Karen,' Ross was saying. 'Jenna is the daughter of my father's third wife. Yvonne is with Alastair at the hospital. We all came back from Paris together.'

Karen looked totally bemused. 'Pleased to meet you, Jenna.' She took Jenna's outstretched hand and dropped it almost immediately. She turned to Ross. 'I don't understand.'

'It's complicated, ' Ross said quickly. 'Suffice to say it's family business. Jenna and I were just about to have a glass of white wine or would you prefer red?'

'No, no, white is fine.'

Jenna stood stiffly in front of the fire, dejected beyond measure that this woman so close to Ross had evidently never heard of her or her mother. But then wasn't that Ross to a T? So private, so introverted, in a damned world of his own. And that was one of the reasons he had always fascinated her so. He had the sort of macho aloofness that drove women wild, wanting to get under his skin, to find the hidden passions.

As she gulped at her wine Jenna wondered if Karen had released those passions as she had once done. She stared down at the rug she was standing on, her rug, Ross's rug. She tried to imagine him and Karen, rolling around...hot and inflamed...

The wine caught the back of her throat and choked her. Ross was at her side immediately, patting her back.

'Are you all right?' he asked with concern.

'It...it went down the wrong way,' she squeaked.

Ross smiled and with his thumb he tenderly rubbed away a drop of wine from her chin. To Jenna's ragged senses he seemed to do it in slow motion. Languorously, and erotically. She felt colour rise to her cheeks at the sexual urge to throw him down on the rug and...

She jerked her chin away and rubbed at it herself. Convinced that he had done it for Karen rather than for her or himself she wondered what sort of a game he was playing. Daring to look at Karen's expression she was sure she was right as the woman's colour had risen but not for the same reasons as hers. Karen looked angry.

'I'll go and check on Charlotte and the supper,' Jenna said quickly. She put her wine glass down on the mantelpiece and scooted from the room, stopping outside the double doors to catch her breath.

'Are you sure she's old enough to drink?' she heard Karen say.

Ross laughed. 'I suspect Jenna could drink you under the table. She lives in Paris and was probably weaned on champagne.'

Jenna flew across the hall, nearly tripping over an

overnight bag at the foot of the stairs. Karen was obviously staying!

It was getting worse. She wished with all her heart she had never come back to England. She wanted to be back in Paris where she should be; expectantly waiting for Marcel's arrival. He hadn't sounded too pleased with her when she had called Spain from Charles De Gaulle airport to tell him she wouldn't be in Paris to welcome him home but was on her way to England instead. Well she was going to make it up to him. She wasn't needed here. Alastair was going to be all right. Yvonne was clearly back on the road to mending her marriage, and Ross? Ross needed her support and presence like he needed a hole in his head!

'Jenna, you're not crying are you?' Ross asked with concern.

She'd never made it to the kitchen. The sight of the dreamboat's overnight bag had had the effect of making her slump against the hall panelling, vowing to bring forward her wedding – she'd marry sooner rather than later!

She rubbed her eyes and forced a sheepish smile. 'Choking on the wine made my eyes water. And I wasn't weaned on champagne by the way,' she added meaningfully.

He raised a dark brow. 'You heard?'

She nodded and made an on-the-spot decision. 'Dinner might be dangerous under the circumstances with your girlfriend's assumption that I'm an under-age drinker, Ross. I might have mellowed over the years but not enough to bite my tongue if she says something like that again.'

Ross laughed, a deep rumble of mirth that made her heart trip painfully. 'You never did stand for a put-down, did you?'

Jenna smiled and Ross lifted her chin with his fingers. 'You look all-in.'

'I did tell you I was tired,' she murmured.

'It's been a wretched day for us all and neither of us got much sleep last night. It was unfair of me to expect you to join us for supper. Go up to bed, Jenna. I'll ask Charlotte to bring you up a tray.'

Jenna hadn't wanted the invitation in the first place but having it lifted from her so unexpectedly wasn't giving her any relief. He clearly didn't want her around and in a perverse way she suddenly wanted to play gooseberry. But that was childish and she was done-in anyway so she didn't protest.

'Goodnight, Ross,' she murmured and went to walk away. He caught her arm and she found herself bound tightly in his arms.

'Thank you for being here, Jenna,' he said softly. 'I couldn't have faced the day without your support.'

His mouth, warm and soft brushed over her lips so tenderly she drew in her breath. And then the pressure deepened and her heart stopped. A kiss of gratitude it wasn't. It was a kiss for a lover, but she wasn't his lover. His lover was waiting expectantly for him in the drawing room. Why was he doing this? And why was she responding, pressing her small hands against his chest but *not* pushing him away.

She did eventually though but not until she heard the kitchen door squeak and it coincided with Ross, rather lazily moving back from her as if it didn't really matter that his housekeeper might see them.

'Goodnight, Jenna,' he murmured and headed back across the hall to the drawing room.

Jenna took off herself, up the stairs, after giving Karen's overnight bag a good kick with her right foot, causing her to wince.

She was desperate to sleep but confusion put paid to that luxury. Why was Ross acting so strangely; kissing her down by the river last night, kissing her again tonight? Did he believe that by doing so that he had the power to stop her marriage? But he *wasn't* against her marriage, her mother was!

And what had those kisses done to her? What did being in the very same room with him do to her? It was tearing her world apart if the truth be known. Just when she had got her life together he was messing it all up for her. It wasn't as if he wanted her for himself. He'd had his chance and blown it.

And tonight he would be sharing a bed with Karen and that was one privilege she had never shared with him. The thought was unbearable.

Jenna was sitting at her old dressing table, pulling a brush through her hair and refusing to acknowledge the image of Ross's face in the reflection behind her – a ghost of the past – when Charlotte bustled into the room with a tray.

'Mr Cameron said you were too exhausted to dine with them tonight. I hope you can manage some of my roast lamb though. It used to be your favourite.'

'Oh, it still is,' Jenna said, striving to sound enthusiastic: not wanting to hurt the kindly housekeeper's feelings. She swivelled round as Charlotte fussed with the tray on a table by the bed.

'Er, Karen, she seems nice. They seem...er... close.' She knew it was unfair to the housekeepers loyalties to probe so, but Jenna was more than curious.

'I wouldn't know, dear. It's none of my business.'

No joy there then. She changed the subject.

'Er, Charlotte. Is Drake still around?'

Drake had always been her favourite of Alastair's stable of horses. Ross rode him on the rare occasions he was down from London but when he wasn't she'd delighted in hacking Drake across the fields. He was a brutish black stallion with a heart of gold once you got to know him.

Charlotte laughed. 'He is indeed. A bit long in the tooth now but Mr Cameron still rides him when he's down. You know your riding stuff is still here.' She threw open one of the wardrobes and Jenna was astonished to see her jodhpurs, boots, hacking jacket and hard hat still hanging there.

Jenna suddenly had the will to ride again. With her mother at Alastair's bedside and Karen at Ross's she could swing herself into the saddle and be away over the fields. Anything to keep out of Ross's space till she made arrangements to leave. She wasn't wanted or needed here. She was going to return to Paris and get on with her wedding plans. With haste.

chapter eight

Jenna dressed quickly and quietly in her riding gear the next morning. It was early and there was no sound of stirring in the house. Before going downstairs she called her mother's mobile and spoke to her for a few minutes asking about Alastair. He'd had a restful night and all was well. Jenna thought how different her mother sounded, as if all her tensions were lifted from her.

It crossed her mind that her mother's strange behaviour towards her wedding plans was linked to her estrangement from Alastair. As Jenna hurried downstairs she hoped that if her mother was reconciled with Alastair she might look on her daughter's forthcoming marriage with more ease and favour.

Jenna made herself a coffee and gazed out of the kitchen window as she sipped it. Already she felt distanced from Paris. Last night she had resolved to leave as soon as was decently possible because in her heart she knew the longer she stayed here the more distanced she would become. And that feeling wasn't right. She should be focused on her marriage to Marcel rather than wasting her time wondering about Ross's relationship with the beautiful Karen!

Determined to rid herself of that particular angst she snatched the stable keys from behind the back door and headed out across the grounds to the paddock and stables. Karen's BMW was still parked at the side of the hall by the garage block but Jenna refused to give it more than a passing glance.

It was a glorious spring day, sunny with a hint of warmth and the gardens looked as pristine as they always did. Spring bulbs were blooming, a wash of yellow and white and the scent of narcissi was heady.

Jenna wished her head was clear enough to appreciate it all fully. She wanted to close herself off for a few hours at least and get some sort of respite after another restless night. Why should it bother her so much that Ross had a woman in his life when she was going to be married anyway? Stop it! Stop it! she resolved.

'Where the devil have you been?' Ross thundered at her when, two hours later, Jenna stepped into the kitchen.

'I'd say that was obvious,' Jenna snapped back at him, flinging her riding hat down on the dresser by the back door and shaking her jet hair free. Drake had been difficult and she hadn't enjoyed her ride as much as she had expected. She'd been disappointed that her beloved Drake hadn't been as enraptured as she at meeting up after three years apart. She'd mastered him in the end but the ride had been a struggle more than a pleasure. Every muscle and sinew in her body ached with strain.

Ross, dressed in chinos and sweatshirt, raked a hand through his hair.

'Stupid question,' he muttered roughly. 'Did...did you ride Drake?'

Jenna raised her dark brows in surprise. 'Of course. Is that a problem?' To Ross it appeared it was. He looked angry and strained.

'Don't do it again, Jenna,' he said thickly. 'You're not strong enough to control him. He isn't fit to ride any more.'

'Charlotte said you still ride him. If he's fit enough for you he's fit enough for me,' Jenna retorted, undoing her jacket and striding past him to the Aga and the coffee pot. She'd ridden all her life and to suggest she was incapable was an insult.

Ross caught her arm and swung her round to face him. His face was taut and pale.

'Jenna, Drake was accidentally shot in the neck last autumn when one of the grooms rode him in the vicinity of a pheasant shoot,' he told her sombrely. 'Not a serious injury but enough to unbalance him. I won't allow anyone near him but myself.'

Jenna went cold inside. 'Well thanks for telling me,' she said rather shakily. 'A bit late but...'

She glanced past him to the wall clock. It was coming up to eight o'clock. She'd been out since six. Two hours riding an unstable stallion who could have spooked at any minute. Nice one Ross!

'I've only just got up. Charlotte said you had asked about Drake last night. I was coming to find you,' Ross breathed heavily.

Jenna, eyes downcast, noticed he was wearing his riding boots. She looked up and saw the deep concern in his eyes and her heart twisted at the sudden realisation that he had been seriously worried about her. Her shoulders sagged as she remembered one of Alastair's riding rules. Always inform someone where you were going before leaving.

'I was OK,' she told him and managed a small smile. 'And thanks for your concern. I didn't know and I didn't think to tell anyone where I was going. I...I just needed to get out and...'

Ross nodded as if he understood but Jenna doubted that he really did. He couldn't know what was going on in her head. She hardly knew herself most of the time.

'I'll make you some breakfast,' he told her and abruptly turned away. 'Charlotte has gone shopping and...'

'And Karen is still in bed,' Jenna finished for him as she shrugged out of her hacking jacket and draped it on the back of a chair.

'I think she's left already,' Ross murmured from the fridge.

Jenna sat down at the long refectory table. 'Don't you know?' she asked rather sarcastically.

Ross turned to her. 'No, I don't know,' he stated thinly. 'Karen didn't share my bed last night if that is what you are thinking.'

He was spot on of course; that was exactly her train of thought. She shifted uncomfortably.

'In fact,' he went on dryly. 'Karen and I don't share a bed anywhere else either. Satisfied?'

Jenna didn't know if she believed him or not, but she had seen the way Karen was with him. Obviously not her choice that the relationship wasn't intimate, if what he said was true. But perhaps it was early days yet. Ross certainly had those passions but...but why an earth was she even giving his sex life a thought?

'Why should I care, Ross?' she tossed back at him flippantly.

'Exactly. Why should you care?' she heard him mutter.

There was silence between them as Ross prepared the breakfast. Jenna moved around the kitchen setting two places and when they both sat down to bacon and eggs, coffee and toast Jenna spoke first, quietly and reasonably.

'Ross, I called my mother this morning before I went out and she said that Alastair is doing well. I think it's clear to us all that there is a reconciliation in the air. They have each other now and you have Karen and well...I'm rather surplus to requirements. If it's all right with you I'd like to return to Paris.'

It seemed that Jenna waited an eternity for his reaction. She watched him lay his fork down and sip at his coffee and when his eyes finally locked onto hers, so fixedly, she felt her insides turn over.

'It isn't all right with me, Jenna. You are *not* returning to Paris.'

His tone was definite, as if the subject was closed for ever. She opened her mouth to speak but no sound came out.

'My father might be out of danger,' he went on, 'but there is another issue to be dealt with, one you seemed to have forgotten. Your wedding plans.'

Jenna closed her eyes in silence for a few seconds. Not all this again. She didn't want another inquisition. When she opened them again she was surprised to see him staring at her throat.

'Why do you still wear my pendant?' he asked thoughtfully.

Instinctively her hand went to the pearl hanging over

the neck of her red cashmere sweater. Why indeed? It caused her more grief than pleasure but it was all she had of him.

'Because it's easy,' she told him and lowered her eyes to her plate. She picked up her fork to try and move some food to her mouth but his hand came over hers to still her.

'Easy?'

'It's a woman's thing, Ross,' she shrugged. 'Some jewellery isn't comfortable to wear. This is. I don't know it's there.' She moved her hand from under his and with both hands undid the catch. 'The sight of it clearly troubles your conscience so I'll take it off. It's history anyway. Satisfied?' she echoed as she tossed the chain and pearl down on the table in front of him.

His mouth was tense and his eyes earnest as he looked at her. When he spoke he spoke softly and meaningfully. 'Your eighteenth birthday will never be history, Jenna. It was a moment of weakness for us both but oddly it is serving me well at the moment.'

Hesitantly Jenna moistened her lips with the tip of her tongue. 'Meaning?'

'Well it poses the question of why you gave yourself willingly to me that night and yet you haven't made love with the man you are supposed to be *in love* with. The man you are proposing to marry.'

Jenna's heart stilled. In anger she had thrown that at him. Admitted that her wedding night would be the first time for her and Marcel. Did Ross have a computer for a brain? He didn't miss a thing.

'Of...of course we've made love,' she protested weakly, averting her eyes from the intensity of his.

Ross shook his head. 'You can't retract now, Jenna. Your last words to me on the morning after we made love were that I was the worst lover you had ever had. We both know I was the *only lover* you had ever had. You lied then and you are lying now. You claim to love Marcel but you haven't made love with him and yet you gave yourself to me: someone you have always despised. It doesn't make sense, Jenna. Not one bit of sense.'

Jenna closed her eyes tightly, dizzy with his painful reminders. Even now, under his drawled accusations she could recall that night with a clarity that dismayed her. The warmth and sexuality of him. Yes, she had given herself willingly and urgently, to drive him towards acknowledging her existence. And he had acknowledged it, loved her very deeply and when he had swept her up into his arms and laid her down in her own bed she had thought it was going to be perfect. But he hadn't come to join her and she had known then that she was nothing in his life and never had been. He had used her and then had the audacity to apologise for it all the next morning; was it any wonder she had fled? She hadn't wanted to hear the rest, the crushing put-down that she meant nothing to him after their impulsive love making.

But that was then, all those miserable years ago, and now he was trying to add more fuel to fire his attempt to stop her marrying. Not for himself, oh, never for himself, but for her *mother*.

'It's when you don't make love to someone that it proves the depth of your love,' she argued faintly. 'I love Marcel so much I want my wedding night to be special and…and he loves me so much he is willing to wait…' She couldn't even admit to herself that she found it slightly disconcerting that she and Marcel had shared nothing more than a few chaste kisses on the cheek or forehead and that Marcel had not pushed for anything more.

Suddenly Ross got to his feet, shoving his chair back from the table. Jenna thought he was going to storm out of the room as her mother often did at the very mention of Marcel. But he didn't. He stood facing her across the table, his features so grave and troubled she wondered what was coming next. He seemed poised to tell her something, something important, because a pulse was throbbing at his throat.

Jenna clasped her hands tightly together in her lap. She felt a peculiar sensation of doom thicken the air around her.

'Jenna,' he murmured thickly. 'I have something to tell you.'

Slowly he moved around the table to her side. Tenderly he took her hands and lifted her to her feet. He held her firmly but gently by her shoulders and looked down into her wide eyes. Jenna stared at him seeing his eyes soften and her heart raced expectantly when he said emotionally. 'I can't stand by and let this marriage happen, Jenna. *I care too much for you and…*'

The urgent bleep of her mobile in the pocket of her hacking jacket sliced through his words. Jenna, transfixed, couldn't respond, she didn't want to. Ross's words were echoing in her head. "I care too much for you". Was it possible that he did? Had her engagement to another man prompted him to realise that life without her was impossible?

Her head swam as the peculiar feeling of impending doom lifted and was gone. She felt lightheaded with expectation but Ross had lapsed into silence. Her mobile persisted. Dazed she reached behind her for her jacket. Fingers trembling she wanted to still it so Ross would go on. She focused her misty eyes on the screen of the phone. She formed a word faintly, 'Paloma'.

Suddenly the phone was taken from her hand as Ross silenced it and slid it across the table, out of reach. Wide eyed she gazed at him and then he reached for her and tenderly took her in his arms.

His kiss was deep and powerful and in that moment Jenna's heart soared. A sob caught in her throat as she clung to him. She was right. Ross *was* jealous and the realisation was ecstatic. Ross cared so deeply for her he was determined to stop her wedding.

Nothing in the world mattered anymore. Safe in his arms Jenna felt all her doubts drain out from her. Relief washed through her till she was weak and senseless and delirious with happiness.

'Oh, Ross,' she breathed raggedly as he lifted his mouth from hers in order to draw breath.

'Jenna, please...' he implored.

His whole body suddenly stiffened and a dreadful, bone-chilling doubt flooded her icily. Was she wrong? Had she misinterpreted his words and actions? Was this a ploy cooked up by him and her mother to unsettle her emotions enough for her to cancel the wedding that everyone was so against?

Ross lifted his hands and cupped her face. Softly he

kissed her suddenly doubtful eyes, her brow, her flushed cheeks.

'Please don't look so frightened my darling,' he whispered into her hair as desperately she clung to him, feeling so very insecure. 'I want to make it all right for you more than anything. There are things you need to know and then and only then can we...'

Suddenly Jenna was out of his embrace, *deja vu* hitting her. She'd been here before, in this very same situation, hearing the very same words. Her eyes narrowed angrily, the disappointment inside her a gruelling ache.

Frowning she stared up at him. She saw what she didn't want to see. Ross's distraught features, his mouth tight lipped, his eyes confused. Not the look of a man who loved her and wanted her, but the look of a man not wanting to commit himself and wondering how to get out of this embarrassing situation.

'Yes, well I think I've heard all that before, Ross,' she told him bluntly, desperately striving for sensibility after letting herself believe that she meant something to him. More fool her.

'Jenna, stop this,' he implored. 'Stop trying to block me when I'm trying to...'

'What, Ross?' she interjected. 'Trying to squirm your way out of another awkward situation you've got yourself into? The last time I was merely a nuisance factor in your life. Someone you had used for carnal satisfaction and wanted to be rid of as soon as possible. But this time it's different. Now you have a new agenda: stop my marriage at whatever cost!'

'Yes, at whatever cost, Jenna,' he breathed wearily.

'But there is more, so much more and you must listen to me.'

'No way, Ross Cameron. You are trying to mess up my head and my emotions every time you take me in your arms and kiss me that way. I've had enough.' In a fury of rejection she snatched at her coat and turned away but paused at the door.

'One last thing. Something you ought to know. You can't stamp on people's emotions and come out unscathed. If you have a conscience take this on board and suffer in hell for it. You broke my heart on the morning after my eighteenth birthday but you will never, *never* do it again.'

She paused to lick her dry lips, tightening her grip on the door till her knuckles whitened. 'You know, Ross, suddenly I understand myself and I have you to thank for it all. I'll admit it. I don't love Marcel, but I'm still going to marry him. He can't hurt me, you see. It's as simple as that.'

She slammed the kitchen door, after giving him a last withering look, but the look he was giving her was one she didn't understand. What an earth had she said to make him to look so relieved?

chapter nine

'You look more in need of this hospital bed than I do, son,' Alastair joked as Ross stepped into his room.

It wasn't surprising. As always after a row with Jenna he felt bruised, but he never failed to rise to the bait when she taunted him. Because he was always so intent on not hurting her he always seemed to end up the loser.

He managed to force a smile for his father. 'It's good to hear that you haven't lost your sense of humour, but if I'm looking a bit frayed at the edges it's all your fault. You gave us all a scare.' He perched himself on the edge of the bed, glad to see his father's colour was back

Alastair chuckled. 'I gave *myself* a scare. A warning the doctor said. Ease up or else. Didn't you bring Jenna with you? I can't wait to see her again after so long. Yvonne told me she was here last night when you all got back from Paris but I guess I was a bit hazy. I don't remember much about yesterday. '

'Jenna wanted to come but I thought you needed more rest. She was disappointed but sends her fondest love,' he told his father.

Ross was sure she would have sent her love if she had known he was coming to the hospital but the rest was a fabrication so as not to unduly concern his father. The truth was Jenna had gone to ground after their breakfast confrontation and who could blame her? He had completely lost the plot. He had tried to tell her the truth about Marcel but, typical of Jenna, she'd taken the wind out of his sails with her biting anger. However at the very least he now had something to work on. She didn't love Marcel. The rest...her admittance that all those years ago he had broken her heart... His conscience had stung more than ever on hearing that and yet at the same time his heart had soared to think she had once cared so much for him.

'Has she mellowed?' Alastair asked with an encouraging twinkle in his eye.

'Changed more than mellowed, father,' Ross laughed lightly.

'And this business with the wedding?'

'Don't concern yourself with it,' Ross insisted calmly. 'Your health is our top priority for the time being.'

'Where's Yvonne?' Alastair asked, looking beyond his son to the door.

Ross smiled, seeing the keen expectation in his father's eye. A reconciliation? Perhaps a good thing under the circumstances.

'She's taking some air in the hospital gardens. I saw her when I arrived.'

'Rotten time for her,' Alastair breathed worriedly. 'What with Jenna and now me.' He smiled suddenly. 'Fate is odd, Ross. This blip with my heart has brought us all back together. I have a feeling Yvonne won't be going back to Paris and hopefully Jenna, with guidance from you, will see the light where her unsuitable fiancé is concerned.'

'We can only live in hope,' Ross nodded with a smile, thinking that the word unsuitable was an understatement in the worst possible way.

'And talking of hope,' Alastair said keenly. 'I hope to get out of here in a few days. I've had a word with the consultant and he'll consider it. Pull a few strings, Ross. I'll make a far speedier recovery in my own surroundings than here.'

'This isn't a situation for pulling strings, father,' Ross laughed. 'There are no problems with the business and all is well at the Hall so just lie there and get well.'

'What about the Maddison site deal? I'm supposed to be there in the morning.'

'It's all in hand, father. And don't let Yvonne hear you talking like that. Don't you ever learn?'

Alastair nodded. 'You're right. I'm getting a second chance in more ways than one. I'd better keep reminding myself of that or I'll be in trouble again. Now you will stay on at the Hall till I've been given the all-clear, won't you?'

'Of course but I will need to go back to London in the next few days.'

'If you must,' Alastair sighed and then brightened. 'Why not take Jenna with you? The change would do her good and perhaps you can talk some sense into her.'

'Enough, father,' Ross insisted as he slid off the bed. 'Everything is under control so concentrate on yourself for once. Is there anything you need?'

'A copy of the *Financial Times* wouldn't go amiss.'

'No chance,' Ross laughed. He leaned over his father

to kiss his brow. Alastair caught hold of his hand and gripped it tightly.

'You haven't done that since you were six,' he growled.

'You haven't had a heart attack before,' Ross told him crisply. 'Now lie there and think of Caribbean cruises when this is all over. I'll send Yvonne in.'

'Give Jenna my love and bring her with you next time,' Alastair called out when Ross reached the door.

'What was that about Jenna?' Yvonne asked as Ross closed the door behind him.

He wondered if she had been hanging around waiting for him in the corridor. 'Dad was just sending his love and hopes to see her soon,' Ross told her, noticing the colour in Yvonne's cheeks and the brightness of her eyes. She seemed in much better shape than the night before when she had been overwhelmed with concern for his father.

Yvonne smiled. 'Yes, you must bring her. Alistair needs to know everyone around him cares. I've just had a word with his consultant and he's confident of a speedy recovery. I assured him that Alistair will get the best possible care at home so hopefully I can take him back to the Hall in a few days time. Till then I shall stay on here with him.'

Ross fought the disturbing feeling of having the rug pulled out from under him. It was he who had picked his father up when Yvonne had walked out on him three years ago. It seemed Yvonne was back and taking over now, as if their estrangement had never happened

'I'm so glad he's going to be all right,' she went on. 'I would never have forgiven myself if...well you know.' She gave a small shudder and then lifted her chin and said brightly. 'Everything is looking so good, Ross. I'm not going to walk out on your father ever again. And now that Jenna is out of Paris and away from...from Marcel...well, life will get back to normal.' She paused, looked thoughtful for a few seconds and then met Ross's eyes.

'Listen, I've been thinking. What we talked about yesterday; I think it's best that Jenna doesn't know the truth about her father, Ross.' She suddenly paled. 'You haven't told her, have you?'

Ross shook his head. 'No, not yet.' But he was getting very close to it and suddenly he didn't like what he was hearing. Yvonne back-tracking again.

'Everything has changed now and nothing will be gained by telling her, Ross. Jenna's home now and she'll soon forget him so it's not necessary to dredge it all up.'

Ross frowned. Taking Yvonne's arm he moved her further up the corridor, away from his father's room where they might be overheard.

'And supposing she doesn't forget him, Yvonne?' he asked her quietly but firmly, inwardly appalled at her naive attitude.

Yvonne looked taken aback. 'But she...she will. She must,' she whispered faintly.

Ross responded sharply, 'Every mention of this wedding has Jenna digging in her heels, Yvonne. Only this morning she said that now Alastair was recovering she wasn't needed and wanted to return to Paris.'

'Don't let her, Ross,' Yvonne implored. 'Do whatever it takes but don't let her go back!'

'And how am I supposed to accomplish that? Declare my undying love, marry her myself and make it easy for you?' Ross shook his head. 'There is only one sure-fire way to end the relationship, Yvonne. The truth, painful as it will be for everyone concerned.'

'No!' Yvonne suddenly snapped. 'You are forgetting something here, Ross; the effect the truth could have on your father.'

Ross looked at her, appalled. Where was her concern for her daughter's feelings? 'This isn't about my father,' he protested. 'This is about Jenna's birthright. She needs to know.'

'If Jenna knows the truth Alastair is sure to find out. This health scare of his changes everything,' she said determinedly. 'He doesn't need further stress in his life.' She lifted her chin defiantly. 'I'm not going to risk losing Alastair over this, Ross.'

'And what exactly do you mean by losing him?' he challenged. 'Do you think he'll be so shocked at your former indiscretion he'll send you back to Paris with disgust?'

The flicker of her lashes suggested that that was exactly what she was thinking, but suddenly she was in control again, with an ice cool gaze that chilled him.

'We used to be friends, Ross but your attitude towards me changed after what I told you about my past. It obviously disgusts you and it will be the same with your father.'

Ross softened. 'No, Yvonne. What happened to you doesn't disgust me and I'm sure my father would be sympathetic but...

'But nothing, Ross,' she insisted. 'I'm adamant that Jenna shall not know and if you have any feelings for your father you will forget everything I told you.' Her eyes narrowed warningly. 'If you don't, Ross, *you* will be to blame if your father suffers another heart attack from the trauma of it all,' she finalised lethally.

Ross's senses reeled under Yvonne's chilling threat. Never would he have thought she could resort to such cruel emotional blackmail to protect herself. Her selfishness astounded him. Drawing a hard breath he knew he couldn't take that lying down.

'Then risk losing your daughter in marriage to her half brother, Yvonne, because I wash my hands of the whole sorry business.'

He turned his back on her and strode down the corridor towards the fresh air that he so badly needed. He heard her call out his name in an agonised cry, but he ignored it.

Outside the hospital he breathed deeply and raggedly. He had no intentions of washing his hands of the whole sorry business but he was determined to let Yvonne stew for a while. Her behaviour was verging on paranoia but she had a point, he had to admit, several points in fact. His father's health was indeed paramount and who knew what effect it would have on him if the truth of Jenna's parentage came out. Ross remembered his own initial reaction, the shock and the pain he had felt for Jenna. His father didn't need that anguish.

And if a miracle happened and Jenna did change her mind about returning to Paris and Marcel; was it necessary for her to know anything about her past?

But how to make that miracle happen? How to keep her here?

On the drive back to the Hall, Ross picked over all Jenna had said this morning, trying to piece it all together. Hearing her admittance that she didn't love Marcel was the only relief he'd felt. The rest had disturbed him. He had broken her heart all those years ago. So she had cared after all and he must have been blind and foolish not to see it at the time. And now she was determined he wouldn't get a second chance to hurt her. But, because of his own sensitivity to her feelings he was incapable of revealing *his* true feelings and, as a result, he was confusing her and she was putting up the barriers.

So did she still care? Jenna was so complex he didn't know what to believe of her half the time. And the complications that came with Yvonne's revelations were a monstrous burden to bear. He felt the overpowering need to tell Jenna the truth about her father, to clear the dross of her past before he committed himself to her future. But was that what she really wanted; a future with him rather than with Marcel?

Well she couldn't have Marcel! It was out of the question. And there was only one way ahead; to find out how deeply Jenna felt for him, Ross, if indeed she cared if at all.

Ross pulled up behind a local taxi in front of the Hall and his blood ran cold. He leapt out of his own car and challenged the cab driver through the open window.

'What do you want?'

'Who do I want?' the driver corrected with a grin. 'A young lady actually. Taxi to the airport, I believe.'

Ross thrust a twenty pound note through the window. 'Change of plan. She's not going anywhere. Thanks for your trouble.'

Heart thundering, Ross leapt up the stone steps. Five minutes later and he might have missed her and all would have been lost. Jenna careered into him as he opened the front door.

'Hey, that's my cab!' she screeched as the taxi disappeared down the drive.

'Not any more,' Ross told her. He took her holdall from her hand and urged her back inside the hall.

'Ross, you can't do this!' Jenna cried hotly. 'I'm going back to Paris.'

'No, you're not. You're staying here with me because we have unfinished business, Jenna. You can't just run away every time things get difficult for you.'

'That's what you think!' she blazed at him, snatching at her bag.

Ross tossed it down on the floor out of her reach and took her firmly by her shoulders. 'I don't want you to go, Jenna. I don't think you want to go either but as always with you, you'd rather cut and run than face up to life.'

'Don't be absurd!' she protested. 'There's no life to face up to here. My life is with Marcel in Paris. I told you that this morning but you never listen.'

'Oh, I listen but what I hear is a muddle of lies more than anything else. First you love Marcel and then you don't. Once I broke your heart but I'll never get a second chance. What does that mean, Jenna? Do you know yourself?'

She shrank under his grip and Ross hated himself for

putting her through this, but he had to get her to open up. He softened his grip on her thin shoulders and softened his tone with it.

'Let me help you, Jenna, because I have failed you before and I don't want to do it again. I didn't know how you felt all those years ago. I was confused myself but I'm not confused any more. I know how I feel about you.'

As soon as she lifted her chin defiantly he knew he was failing yet again. Why couldn't he just come out with it and say how deeply he loved her? But that lurking knowledge of what he knew about her past was clouding the issue this time. It was almost as if he would be declaring his love in order to save her.

'Go on then, Ross,' she suddenly murmured. 'Tell me exactly how you feel about me.'

She held his eyes but not with the warmth he needed to see to urge him to open up his heart. He sensed this was a challenge, some sort of a test. But if he didn't give an answer she would have triumphed yet again. It was pride, he knew; an insufferable quirk of his nature which he wished he didn't possess. In business he did not put himself into situations where failure was a possibility. He'd learned that from his father. But this was an emotional thing, something he was a complete and utter novice at, and fear of rejection held him back.

'You can't say it, can you, Ross?' Jenna went on, so quietly and despondently that he barely heard her. 'You can't say it because you don't feel it.' She jerked her shoulders from his grasp and took a step back. 'Oddly enough you have gone up in my estimation for that. I know what you're trying to do, Ross,' she went on smoothly. 'You've just come back from the hospital and you've talked with my mother and...'

'This has nothing to do with your mother, Jenna,' he interrupted. 'This is about us.'

She shook her head. 'No, it isn't. It's about my mother's opposition to my wedding. She called me, you see, when you were on your way home. She told me about your little chat in the corridor outside your father's sick-room. It disgusted me so much I slammed the phone down on her.'

Ross stiffened, his heart twisting. Yvonne had confessed all, over the phone, not face to face with her daughter! Jenna knew about her father and Marcel! Now he understood her need for flight. But back to Paris? Surely that should be her last place of refuge under the circumstances?

He reached for her again, to hold her and reassure her, but she put more space between them with another backwards step.

'It won't work, Ross. Whatever you say I will always know that you don't mean it.' Suddenly she let out a small laugh and shrugged her shoulders helplessly. 'Just now, when you were on the verge of saying you cared I was amazed to think that you would go that far to please my mother. Dismayed but fascinated all the same. Why, Ross, why?'

Ross frowned, suddenly confused. 'Jenna, what an earth are you talking about?' Suddenly he had the feeling he was on the wrong track here. Perhaps Yvonne hadn't confessed all and yet...

'I'm talking about your willingness to sacrifice your

freedom for me, Ross, that's what I'm talking about. My mother told me that you'd said you loved me and wanted to marry me. And I suppose in your arrogance you thought I would accept. Get real, Ross. Did you honestly think I would seriously consider marrying you instead of Marcel?'

'What!' Ross shouted, mentally reeling as if he had been struck by a bolt of lightening.

Jenna laughed again but the sound had a painfully hollow ring to it. 'Don't act so surprised that your intentions have been thwarted, Ross. You love me even less than Marcel does so you are not even in the running. I'll despise you and my mother ever more for this. Together you've cooked up this plot to stop my marriage and it's nothing short of cruel.'

Realisation hit Ross where it hurt, deep, deep in his heart. Yvonne had used his very own words, thrown at her so flippantly and sarcastically, a hypothetical reason to stop Jenna's wedding plans, as a deadly weapon in her scheme. *Declare my undying love, marry her myself.* Oh, the folly of sarcasm, the folly of a careless choice of words. As Jenna had so wisely said, how could she ever believe anything he said again?

'You have it all wrong,' he attempted, dragging a hand through his hair. 'There is no plot. It was an impetuous remark made in the heat of an argument. God dammit, Jenna, your mother will use any weapon she can get hold of to stop your marriage to Marcel.'

'Whatever – she has failed and so have you. To hell with you, Ross. You might have thought your were being noble in trying to stop my marriage to a man my mother doesn't approve of by marrying me yourself, but it's pathetic!'

She turned and, grabbing her bag from the floor, flew up the stairs.

Ross stood motionless, his fists clenched tightly at his side. His anger against Yvonne a ball of fire inside him, consuming him. She'd ruined it all, damn her! What chance did he have of winning Jenna now?

chapter ten

Jenna banged the bedroom door behind her, dropped her bag and leaned back against the door. She drew in several deep breaths and tried to calm of her senses.

Damn it! If only that taxi had arrived earlier. She would have missed Ross and been well on her way to the airport by now. But he had caught her when she hadn't wanted to face him after what her mother had told her, not ever again!

And instead of grabbing her bag and rushing out of the front door she had run upstairs to her bedroom! Was she mad?

Frantically she fumbled in her pocket, pulled out her mobile and tried to remember the phone number of the cab company, but it had vanished from her muddled brain. In frustration and despair she threw the phone across the room where it hit the wall and clattered to the floor. Oh, why had Ross come back when he had? Why couldn't he just leave her alone to get on with her life?

She felt the door move behind her and she braced herself against it to keep him out.

'Go to hell, Ross! I've just called another cab and you won't stop me leaving this time!' she yelled out.

'Jenna, it's me, Charlotte. I've brought you some coffee.'

Jenna moved away from the door, embarrassed down

to her toes. Charlotte opened the door and came into the bedroom with a tray of coffee and biscuits.

'I would have thought you'd have grown out of those childish tantrums by now, Jenna,' she laughed as she placed the tray on the dressing table. 'Mr Cameron said to bring this up for you. Excuse me prying but did you say you were leaving?'

Raking her hair back from her brow Jenna nodded. 'Yes, I am. I...I *was* going to say goodbye, Charlotte.'

Charlotte looked disappointed. 'But you've only just got here. I was so looking forward to having you stay. If you have to go you must, but it's a terrible shame. Your mother rang me earlier to say she could be bringing Mr Cameron home in a few days. It would have been so nice to have the whole family back together again.'

In everyone's dreams but mine, Jenna thought despondently.

'Er, yes, well I have things to do in Paris,' she managed to murmur.

'Yes, Jenna is going to be married, Charlotte,' Ross said from the doorway. He was carrying a spare cup and saucer and walked straight into the room. With the housekeeper there Jenna couldn't stop him.

But it didn't stop her shooting him a poisonous look. Charlotte looked startled. Ross was quick on the uptake.

'Don't look so surprised, Charlotte. There is a man out there somewhere willing to marry her!'

Charlotte blushed. 'Oh, Mr Cameron, I wasn't thinking anything of the sort.'

Ross smiled and patted her shoulder in passing. 'I

know you weren't, Charlotte. It's my warped sense of humour at play.'

Jenna pulled herself together. 'Since when have you had *any* sense of humour, Ross?' she retorted sharply.

Charlotte chuckled and shook her head. 'Oh, it's just like old times. You two were always at each other's throats.' She stopped at the door. 'My very best wishes to you, Jenna, dear. He'll be a lucky man to have such a beautiful bride. Don't forget to come and see me before you leave.' She shut the door quietly behind her.

Angrily Jenna glared at Ross as he poured two cups of coffee. 'Your arrogance knows no bounds, Ross. Using your housekeeper to have a dig at me. How low can you get?'

'Lower than that if needs be,' he muttered. He handed her a cup of coffee and gazed levelly at her. 'It's true anyway. You *are* returning to Paris to be married, aren't you?'

Jenna lifted her chin. 'Of course. I haven't had a better offer so why shouldn't I?' she mumbled sarcastically.

'So my offer of marriage is definitely rejected, is it?' He shrugged without waiting for an answer. 'Well you win some and you lose some. That's life!'

Gulping down her coffee Jenna wondered what sort of game Ross was playing now.

'So you concede defeat?' she managed faintly.

'I concede,' he admitted with a nonchalant shrug. 'Funny – failure isn't as bad as I thought it might be. But then if the stakes aren't very high, what's the loss?'

Jenna slammed her coffee cup down on the tray with

a clatter, astounded by his sudden flippancy. 'Will you stop this, Ross?'

'Stop what?' he responded in all innocence. 'I'm only trying to make it easier for you. I'll even drive you to the airport if you can stand my company a little longer.'

Jenna's heart slowed dangerously. Why this sudden turn around in his thinking? He'd been determined to ruin her marriage prospects and now he was practically throwing her out of the door to get on with it! Suddenly she got the message.

She smiled knowingly. 'Ah, I see what is going on here. You think by saying the opposite of what you want me to do I'll go completely the other way. You can't change my mind with your devious little tricks, Ross.'

Ross leaned back against the dressing table, folded his arms across his chest and shook his dark head.

'You've got it all wrong, Jenna. I was never against this marriage from the start, if you remember rightly. Admittedly I wavered a bit along the way because I'm morally opposed to marriage without love. But it doesn't seem to bother *you*, so go ahead.'

Her mouth was suddenly dry. She hadn't expected any of this. He was giving her her freedom and it was exactly what she wanted, especially after what her mother had told her, but she felt dead inside all the same.

'You quote morals but yours live under a stone,' she told him. 'You and my mother tried to conspire to break up my marriage plans with another plan. You instead of Marcel as the groom.'

'There was never a plan, Jenna. Your mother misinterpreted my words and used them to her advantage. Do you honestly believe I would ever go along with such a conspiracy?'

No, she hadn't, not at first. When her mother had told her, her stupid heart had leapt wildly with hope, only to be dashed when thinking about it good and hard and finally coming to her senses. If Ross had any such feelings for her he wouldn't allow them to be announced by a third party. That wasn't his style. The conspiracy theory had taken root. That wasn't Ross's style either but maybe under the circumstances of his father's illness he would do *anything* to ease Yvonne's concerns and organise a quiet life for everyone. With those thoughts whirling around her brain she had cried, "nonsense" at her mother and banged the phone down on her.

Her doubts had finally been confirmed when Ross had caught her fleeing. She'd tried to push him to reveal his real feelings but there was little point because Ross didn't have any real feelings where she was concerned.

'You did just now,' she retorted. 'You asked me if I was definitely rejecting you and then you conceded defeat with a shrug of your shoulders. There *was* a conspiracy, Ross, and it failed. You can't deny it.'

'I can and I will because it's the truth. Just now I was simply going along with you. You never did listen so I'm done with trying anymore. You wear me out, Jenna.'

He pushed himself away from the dressing table as Jenna slumped down on the edge of her bed, her head bowed. She could feel everything slipping away from her. All hope where Ross was concerned. Her heart was hurting more than it ever had in her life.

She heard the clink of china and lifted her head to

look at the man she could never have. He had his back to as he her piled their coffee cups onto the tray but she saw his grave features reflected in the mirror. She wished with all her heart that she could turn the clock back and that this was the morning after the most wonderful night of her life. The night of Ross's complete and utter surrender to her. She shouldn't have walked out on him in anger but she hadn't learned much since. She was still running and still angry with him most of the time.

'Ross,' she whispered plaintively. 'What exactly did you say to my mother for her to think that you wanted to marry me?'

Ross let out a deep sigh and leaned back against the dressing table. He looked at her, held her eyes with his and spoke very tenderly.

'Jenna, your mother doesn't approve of Marcel,' he began as if he was telling her something she didn't know already. 'She appealed to me not to give up on persuading you out of this marriage. I told her that there was nothing I could do as you were determined to go through with it. She got upset. I asked what she expected me to do...marry you myself? I didn't mean it. I was angry. Your mother used my flippant words in desperation, Jenna.'

Jenna closed her eyes tightly. She had pushed for this explanation, but now she had heard it she wished she hadn't. What an earth was her mother thinking off in saying such things? Why was Yvonne using Ross to dissuade her own daughter out of marriage when she ought to be doing it herself?

Without looking at Ross she murmured. 'And she *is*

desperate, isn't she? Using you this way and clutching at every conceivable straw to get what she wants.'

She blinked her eyes open and found Ross watching her intently, his eyes a darker blue than she had ever seen them before.

'Perhaps now you realise how unhappy you are making her, Jenna?' he asked softly. 'Is it all worth it? You admit yourself that you don't love Marcel.'

Jenna shook her head. 'I want to get married, to settle down. Why should I give up Marcel for my mother, Ross?'

'Because you love your mother and you *don't* love Marcel.'

Jenna's eyes widened. 'That's a cruel thing to say, Ross. You're trying to make me choose and it's not about choice. I'm ready for marriage. It's what I want.'

'Marry me then.'

Jenna felt as if she had been stabbed with a very sharp object. She physically flinched with pain. 'Why on earth would I do that, Ross?' she blurted out angrily.

Ross shrugged as if they were discussing nothing more serious than the state of the weather.

'What difference will it make *who* you marry, Jenna? You just said you are ready for it. You don't love Marcel so why not me?'

Shooting to her feet, Jenna stood trembling by the bed, her nails painfully digging into the palms of her hands 'Th...that is absurd reasoning, Ross! Absolutely bizarre!'

'It isn't at all,' he reasoned calmly. 'Your mother thoroughly approves of me. My father would be over the moon and I rather think Charlotte would be happy with the arrangement.'

'Damn you, Ross,' Jenna blazed. 'You are treating all this is as if it's a joke!'

Ross narrowed his eyes intently. 'I'm deadly serious, Jenna. Marriage is a serious matter and...'

'Exactly!' she cried vehemently. 'Too serious for you to make crazy promises over. You're not the marrying kind. You said it yourself, only last night. You're not an impulsive man, Ross, and this silly, silly proposal *is* an impulse. When have you ever done anything in your life that wasn't measured and controlled? Never, Ross. Never!'

He stepped towards her and Jenna shrank back. She held up her palms to ward him off in case she couldn't control herself and lashed out at him. This was a cruel and wicked argument. The suggestion that she marry him to make everyone else happy was a solution he actually seemed to believe would work.

'I did act on impulse once, Jenna, as you know,' he reminded her darkly.

He stopped in front of her and weakly she let her hands drop to her sides.

'Don't remind me,' she breathed anxiously.

'Why shouldn't I? If I did it once I'm capable of doing it again, but don't look so alarmed. I'm not thinking of throwing you down on the bed and repeating history.'

'Thanks for small mercies,' she breathed sarcastically. 'My relief is immeasurable. Now let's get back to this other impulse of yours.' She narrowed her eyes at him. 'I wouldn't dream of marrying you, Ross,' she stated firmly.

He smiled. He actually smiled! 'Which brings me back to my original question. Why not? On your own admission you weren't planning to marry Marcel on the basis of love and he for sure doesn't love you...'

'I didn't say that!'

'Not exactly but I am capable of reading between the lines of everything you say. Just then you said that I love you even less than he does, so I wasn't in the running. I guess that confirms my feelings that it would be a marriage of convenience more than anything else.'

Jenna bit hard on her bottom lip. Half the time she couldn't remember what she did say to him but it was true. Although Marcel had proposed to her, it hadn't come with passion in his heart. She was under no illusions as to his reasons for marriage. He wanted to stabilise his life for his father and settling down with her would have done that. Her reasons for accepting were similar, stability and security: something she had always lacked in her life. Marriages had succeeded on less.

Jenna sighed in frustration. 'True, I *was* willing to go through a marriage without love,' she admitted.

'But you won't do it with me?'

Jenna's heart flattened. If that wasn't confirmation that he didn't care a jot for her she didn't know what was. Taking hold of her bruised senses she stiffened her shoulders.

'Get out, Ross,' she breathed heavily. 'I don't want to hear any more of your twisted reasoning. You've got what you wanted, the truth. I was considering a marriage without a meaningful basis but nothing has changed.'

'Nothing has changed because you still haven't

answered my question. Why not marry me instead? Do you need further help to come to a decision?'

This time there was no escape. He was on top of her before she could stop him. He slid his arms around her waist and urged her hard against him. She tried to twist her head away from him but he was too quick for her.

His mouth was on hers in an earth shattering kiss which made her senses swim cruelly. Her hands came up against his chest and her fingers clawed into his shirt. Desperately she wanted him to stop because already the rush of arousal took precedence over the deep emotional pain he was inflicting upon her.

How could she give him an honest answer when it would give away her feelings?

Yes, she had been willing to marry a man she didn't love but the thought of marrying Ross was impossible because she *did* love him. *And he didn't love her*. She wouldn't be able to suffer the agony of that.

His hand slid under her soft sweater and his kiss deepened with his heightened arousal as he caressed her bare skin. Jenna moaned and clung to him and momentarily savoured the pressure of his lips on hers because she knew it had to end.

'No, Ross, please don't...' she moaned and struggled to be free of him.

He was too strong for her. One arm held her like a vice while the other came up to her chin to force her to face him.

'Why not, Jenna?' he said in a deep low voice, his eyes narrowed questioningly. 'You didn't say no the last time I made love to you. You pleaded for me not to stop.'

'It's different now!' she cried, her eyes filling with tears. She balled her fists and pushed at his chest. 'I had nothing to lose and everything to gain then, Ross. I gambled my innocence in the hope of winning your heart but I lost out. You didn't want me then and you don't want me now! You're breaking my heart all over again which proves that you don't care for me in any way.'

She tried to pushed him harder but he was a like rock in front of her. His grip on her softened though and he released her chin and nuzzled his lips against her hair.

'If I'm breaking your heart again then you do care for me after all,' he murmured thickly. 'Yet you won't marry me.'

It took all of Jenna's strength to tear herself out of his arms. Bereft she faced him finding the strength from deep inside herself. She had nothing to lose anymore. She wasn't full of pride like him. *She* could face her demons.

'No I won't marry you for the very reason that I *do* care.' She licked her moist lips and her voice grew stronger. 'You don't love me, Ross and that would be worse than a marriage between *two* people who don't love each other. It would work for me and for Marcel because there is nothing at stake, nothing to lose and maybe in time our marriage would give me some sort of satisfaction. But marriage to you would give me no joy, only grief. Every morning of my married life I would look at you with despair because you can't return the feelings that I have for you!'

'I never said I would marry you without love, Jenna,' Ross said tenderly and took her hands in his and squeezed them tightly.

Confused, tears blurring her eyes she tried to focus on his face.

'You presume so much and understand so little, my darling,' he was saying as Jenna's head started to spin. 'If I did lead you to believe I didn't care it was only to make you mad enough to open up your heart to me. You so often speak in anger. I adore you, Jenna. I loved you all those years ago but I was too confused to admit it. I love you now and at last I can admit it because I'm not confused anymore.'

Jenna's hands went to cover her face where her tears flowed freely. Was this a dream? Would she open her eyes and find him a figment of her imagination and his words a fantasy she had always longed to hear? Slowly Ross took her hands away from her face and kissed her burning cheeks.

'Never will I let you slip out of my grasp again, Jenna, my love,' he whispered sincerely. 'You're mine now and you always will be.'

He sought her lips and at last Jenna gave them willingly. Ecstatic with sudden happiness she tightened her arms around him and felt every last vestige of anguish slide out from her. He had opened his heart at last and it was all hers. So long she had waited and now it was all over and she was where she was destined to be. In the arms of the man she loved more than life itself and who loved her just as deeply.

As he lifted her onto the bed she knew he would still be there later, holding her and telling her everything she wanted to hear because this time it was different.

chapter eleven

Last time had been frantic; an erotic coupling born out of anger and frustration and shocking in its raw intensity. Now it was a sweet ecstasy born out of a long awaited declaration of love, and yet still as exciting and enthralling as the first time. Long silken strokes of new discovery and deeper and deeper feelings of need.

There was time to relish every touch, to swim in the deliciousness of loving so deeply and then as the fire expanded, engulfing them both, passion took over.

Their breathing quickened. Jenna responded urgently to his magical touch and yet her senses felt drugged, as if they were soaring away without her. Her skin was on fire, burning where he touched and then cooling as his mouth provoked the most intimate part of her. Heat again and a soft moan of ecstasy as she felt him press fervently between her legs. Clinging to him she pulled him into her and was lost in the oblivion of love with the only man in the world she had ever wanted to possess so thoroughly.

Hearts, souls and bodies melded and moved and thrust till they were gasping with passion and then the roaring heat of a climax that had them both crying out, grasping at each other, joined in an explosion of release, hot and wild and so deeply penetrating.

And through the blur of her slowing heartbeat and the rush of love that flooded her body Jenna felt a wonderful calmness that had eluded her till now. She lay in Ross's arms, listening to his breath levelling and the thud of his heartbeat and knew that at last she had the only man she had ever wanted. Ross was hers, hers to love and cherish and the feeling was sublime.

'Did we sleep?' she murmured later, blinking open her eyes and seeing him gazing down at her.

Ross kissed her lips thoroughly and then drew back. 'You did,' he whispered through a smile, 'but I love you so much I didn't want to waste a moment of looking at you.'

Lightly she ran her fingers down the side of his face. She'd never been so happy. 'This isn't a dream, is it?'

He laughed softly. 'No, my darling, it's for real and I'm still here.'

'I knew you would be this time,' she murmured and twisted her arms possessively around his neck, wanting to stay like this forever.

They lay for a while, wrapped in each others arms, wrapped in their love.

At last Ross spoke, bringing her out of her trancelike state. 'Jenna, there is something you have to do,' he told her quietly.

She was dismayed to see him looking quite serious. Her heart flinched and it must have shown in her face because he smiled reassuringly.

'Don't panic, my love, it's something you *have* to do but it could be somewhat unpleasant for you.'

Ross pushed the covers back and slid his legs out of the bed. Jenna sat up and clasped her knees to her chin to watch him pensively as he pulled his shirt around his shoulders.

'I'm so happy I can't imagine anything unpleasant happening in my life ever again.'

Turning to her Ross smiled adoringly. 'That's the nicest compliment I've ever received.' He stood up and leaned over her to kiss the top of her head. 'I hate to have to bring reality to bear, my darling, but you have to call Marcel,' he said softly but firmly.

Jenna's heart sank like a stone. 'Oh,' she sighed, wishing Ross hadn't burst her bubble of happiness quite so soon.

Raking her hair back from her face she felt a stab of guilt for not having thought of Marcel before Ross had. He was right, of course; she had to break off her engagement immediately. Despondently she slipped out of bed to dress. Fastening her jeans she muttered. 'I suppose what we have just done could be classed as adultery.'

'You're not about to go on a guilt trip, are you?' Ross asked with a low laugh.

Jenna shrugged helplessly. 'I think I must be. I am engaged to be married after all.'

Ross turned and took her left hand and kissed it lightly. 'In theory I suppose, but you don't wear an engagement ring.'

Jenna laughed hesitantly and drew her hand back. 'Funny you've never mentioned it before. I would have thought you'd have jumped on its absence sooner.'

'I didn't notice actually,' Ross admitted. 'So much else has been going on.'

'I have got one though, Ross.'

'Don't tell me, it's not an easy piece of jewellery to wear,' he laughed and gathered her into his arms.

'You wear my pendant though; I did notice that and I'm flattered.'

She linked her arms around his neck. 'Not any more. You forced me to throw it back at you.' She smiled at him seductively. 'Can I have it back now?' she asked.

He kissed the tip of her nose. 'Not till you break off your engagement,' he teased. 'Anyway, what sort of an engagement is it if he bought you a ring that isn't comfortable to wear?'

'I didn't say it was uncomfortable,' she laughed, 'but it was slightly too big. Marcel took it to a jewellers to be made smaller.'

She kissed him lightly in return and sat down on the bed to slip on her loafers.

'It belonged to his mother who left his father when Marcel was small. A beautiful emerald with diamonds. Although it was very lovely I wasn't too happy accepting it, but Marcel said as we had so much in common, me not ever knowing my real father and him not remembering his mother; it seemed right somehow.'

Jenna stood up to pull her sweater over her head. 'It never seemed right to me, *somehow*,' she mused. 'Gerard told Marcel when he was old enough to know that his mother had left them because she'd found out he was having an affair with a student when Marcel was a baby. It broke up the marriage and Gerard has never forgiven himself for his stupid indiscretion as he truly loved his wife. Sad, isn't it?'

She looked up to see Ross, pale-faced, watching her intently, his hands stilled on the leather belt at his waist.

She frowned with concern, wondering what she had said to startle him so. 'What's wrong?'

'I...I don't like hearing about Marcel,' he said quickly. 'You've never said much about him before and...'

'And you're jealous?' she queried softly, secretly pleased that he was.

He pinched the bridge of his nose. 'Jealousy is new to me, Jenna, and yes, I guess it's what I'm feeling because it's beginning to sound as if you were closer to him than I thought.'

Jenna went to him quickly and took his hands and entwined her fingers with his to reassure him. 'Ross, you are the one I'm deeply in love with. Yes, I was prepared to marry Marcel but only because I couldn't have you. Marcel and I had a past in common and a few other things besides. We got on well together and I thought that would be enough to start us off but I know that to be impossible now.'

'And Marcel?' he said thickly. 'Neither of us have given much thought to his feelings at all. He gave you his mother's ring for goodness sake! That shows a depth of feeling that you seem to have missed.' He pulled his hands from hers and snatched his tie up from the floor. His features were so grave Jenna felt a thread of uncertainty run through her veins. It resulted in a show of defence.

'Well who's on a guilt trip now!' she suddenly flamed at him. 'Pity you didn't think of Marcel's feelings before coming to Paris to break up our engagement.'

'Don't start a row, Jenna,' he clipped. 'We're only five minutes into the rest of our lives and it doesn't bode well for the future.'

Jenna chewed nervously on her bottom lip and tried to stay calm. This was certainly no way to start their lives together but she wasn't going to let Ross get away with trying to push her somewhere she didn't want to be: at the bottom of a pit of guilt over Marcel.

'I'm not starting a row, Ross. But suddenly you are trying to make me feel guilty about Marcel and it's working. I don't want to feel that way. I was never under the illusion that Marcel proposed to me for any other reason than that he wanted to stabilise his life for his father's career, but you are making me feel that it could go deeper for him. Thanks a bunch! I'm the one who has to go back to Paris and face him, not you!'

Ross swung around to face her. He looked dumbfounded. 'What do you mean, go back to Paris?'

In exasperation Jenna glared back it him.. 'I have to, Ross,' she insisted. 'I can't just pick up the phone and say, sorry, chéri, the wedding is off. It's not the sort of thing to do over the phone.

His eyes darkened angrily. 'It's exactly the sort of thing to do over the phone, Jenna. It was that sort of an engagement!

''Whatever sort of an engagement it was it doesn't deserve to be dismissed so lightly, Ross,' Jenna reasoned. 'Marcel and I were in a relationship and at this moment he still thinks we are.'

'Some relationship, Jenna,' he said scathingly. 'Tell me, has he called you since you've been here?'

'Well, no,' she reluctantly admitted.

'And have you called him since your arrival here?'

'Well, no, but then there have been more important

things on my mind,' she argued hotly. 'Your father's health and...and...'

'And riding Drake this morning,' he interjected, raising his dark brows questioningly. 'To say nothing of bedding me just now.'

'OK, OK! Point taken. Don't make me feel even worse about it all.'

Damn him, he was right. Marcel hadn't even called to see if she had arrived safely, least of all to ask about her stepfather's health. And she was so wrapped up in herself *she* hadn't given a thought to Marcel.

'So, it's settled,' Ross said firmly. 'You are not returning to Paris and that's final.'

She would have to at some time and so would her mother. They had their home of three years to sort out but she didn't thrust that on Ross. It could wait but there was something that couldn't. If he thought it acceptable to make demands on her she could do likewise.

'It works both ways, Ross,' she started. 'If you insist on me not going to Paris to face Marcel then you can pick up the phone and break it off with Karen.'

'What!'

Jenna folded her arms over her chest quite enjoying this new role of the demanding wife-to-be. Ross was looking totally flabbergasted.

'Phone Karen and tell her you don't want to see her anymore,' Jenna told him firmly. 'You are quick enough to get me to end it with Marcel, so you can do the very same thing for me.'

'But Karen doesn't mean anything to me, Jenna.' Ross started to laugh in disbelief and raked his fingers through his hair. 'She's more of a companion than anything else.'

'A companion, eh?' she growled sarcastically, her eyes suddenly twinkling. 'Sounds quaintly old-fashioned but I very much doubt she sees the relationship in quite the same way. She was here like a shot when your father was taken ill *and* she arrived with an overnight bag *and* she flung her arms around you very intimately *and* she tried to put me down in your eyes.'

Ross's eyes softened and the corner of his mouth twitched. 'And now you are jealous.'

'Huh. Don't look so triumphant about it, Ross. It's no big deal.'

'My relationship with Karen is no big deal either, Jenna.'

'Then it should be easy enough to end,' she giggled back at him.

He came and took her in his arms again and he was smiling. 'I'm beginning to wonder what I've let myself in for in loving you,' he murmured.

'I doubt it will be a quiet life, Ross,' she laughed lightly and sought his mouth.

'When was it ever with you in the house,' he breathed into her neck after kissing her deeply. 'Truce. Let's limit ourselves to only one argument a day. I don't think my blood pressure will allow for more.'

'Spoilsport,' she laughed. 'You'll deprive me of one of my greatest pleasures in life, driving you to distraction.'

'You only get a kick out of it because you know where it leads,' he teased, running his hands over her breasts. Suddenly he dropped his hands to her waist, turned her away from him and gave her a gentle shove. 'Off, with you. You're too much of a temptation. You have ten minutes, darling. Call Marcel and end it because your engagement is driving a wedge between us and I want it over with. Then we're leaving.'

In surprise Jenna swung back to face him. 'To the hospital to tell your father and my mother our news?' she breathed excitedly. She couldn't wait to tell them.

Jenna thought Ross's sudden laugh came over as slightly hesitant.

'Let's not rush things, Jenna.' He sighed and lifted her chin. 'Don't look at me that way, suddenly so doubtful and disappointed. I love and adore you and I'm as eager as you to share our happiness but they are rather wrapped up in themselves at the moment so let them enjoy their own time and space together as we are going to do.'

He kissed her lips softly. 'We're leaving for London for a few days,' he told her. 'My father made the suggestion and I think it's a good one. I have a meeting I need to attend and some directors to direct and you can shop till you drop and the rest of the time will be ours. Do you mind?'

'I'd love to go to London with you,' she murmured happily.

'I have a couple of calls to make before we leave and I have to tell Charlotte our change of plans.' He smiled. 'She'll be pleased to hear you aren't leaving.'

'And will you tell her the reason?' she teased.

'Without telling my father and your mother first? I don't think so!' he laughed and then his brow suddenly creased with concern. 'I need to call your mother too.

I left her on rather an unpleasant note and have to apologise for it.' He smiled suddenly. 'Now make that call of yours, before you forget.'

Sinking down onto the crumpled bed after Ross had left the room Jenna was alone with her thoughts. She was ecstatically happy but rather wished Ross wasn't so keen to throw himself back into his work quite so soon. He'd sounded very much like Alastair just now.

But she was determined not to be like her mother and make unfair demands on Ross's time. He had to make a living, after all, and…and she had a phone call to make, she thought with despondency.

She found her mobile under the chest of drawers by the wardrobe. Mercifully it had remained intact after she had flung it across the room. She stared at it for a long time, uncertain of what to say to end it all. Being engaged to Marcel had been easy, they had just sort of slipped into it. Slipping out of it seemed a Herculean task at the moment. How an earth had she got herself into this mess in the first place? she asked herself but instantly knew the answer.

All her life she had wanted security and for most of her life she had wanted that security with Ross, but it had all gone wrong. Marcel had seemed to be a gift from the gods, an opportunity to put the past behind her. Undemanding in most respects he would have made a good partner. How could she have ever thought she could cope with the more intimate side of marriage, though? There had only ever been Ross.

With the warmth of Ross's love wrapped around her she knew she had to do what he asked. It gave her strength. Decisively she punched out Marcel's cell phone number. Absurdly she felt relieved when there was no reply. She tried his studio. No reply. His apartment, a recorded message. She declined to leave one. It was bad enough that she had to do this over the airwaves; on a recorded message it would be ten times worse.

Angrily she gave up. Ross was right, it was a wedge between them and she silently cursed Marcel for not being available to make it easier for her.

Gathering up her already packed holdall she felt a thrill of excitement at the thought of going to London with him. She'd never been to his Knightsbridge apartment. It was a part of him she didn't know and she adored London any way. She just wished she could have spoken to Marcel first instead of having her engagement still hanging over her like a black cloud in an otherwise bright blue sky.

chapter twelve

'Are you happy, Jenna?' Ross asked.

Over the past three days he wouldn't have thought to ask but today was different. Seated at his desk on the other side of the sitting room of his sixth floor apartment he'd pushed his paperwork aside to watch her as she sat huddled on the wide window seat gazing blindly out of the window as he worked.

London suited her. She had been radiant since their arrival. Inadvertently he had found himself caught up with more work than he had anticipated but she hadn't murmured a word of complaint. She'd flown around town and found plenty to do in his absences. And when they were together every minute was precious, their love and devotion to each other so complete they couldn't have been happier.

They had existed in a vacuum. Ross had blanked out the devastating revelation Jenna had made about her engagement ring. She had told him so innocently, without knowing that it had been her very own mother who had broken up Marcel's parent's marriage. The very thought had sickened him and strengthened his resolve to abide by Yvonne's wishes to keep the whole sordid business a secret. He had to concede that she was right. No good would come from Jenna knowing. And now that he and Jenna were going to be married what did the past matter?

But tonight when he had returned home he had sensed that all was not well with Jenna. True she had thrown herself into his arms as soon as he had stepped through the door but she'd felt different, tense in his arms.

'Of course. Aren't you?' she replied softly without turning to look at him.

She was wearing a sloppy T-shirt and floppy pants and barefoot she looked so refreshingly young and innocent that his heart ached with love for her.

Ross got up, went to her and sat down and took her small feet in his hands. They felt hot, he blew on them so that she laughed and curled her toes.

'That's better,' he smiled. 'Now what's wrong? There's something on your mind. Are you cross with me for spending too much time away from you?'

She fluttered her lashes at him and smiled but Ross sensed she'd had to force it.

'Of course not, silly. I know that you would much rather be with me than at your rotten old office. I'm not like my mother you know. She really resented Alastair working so hard and leaving her alone much of the time.' She sighed. 'I...I'm just feeling a bit tired tonight.'

Ross nodded. 'London can be tiring.' He kissed her hand. 'Let me run you a bath and while you soak I'll rustle up some supper. We'll have a quiet night in.'

As he got up Jenna snatched at his hand and squeezed it. 'Ross, I want to go home,' she pleaded.

Ross froze, his heart thudding in his chest. His thoughts went haywire. So this was what was troubling her. Had she been feeling like that since she had phoned

Marcel to break off their engagement? Had Marcel managed to persuade her that *he* was the one for her and not anyone else? She'd lived a lie with him for three days, loving *him* so completely and yet in the back of her devious little mind plotting to return to Marcel.

'I won't allow you to return to Paris, Jenna,' he told her icily. 'Never.'

Jenna shot to her feet and gripped his arms. 'I meant *our* home, Ross, not Paris. Amersham Hall. My mother called this morning and Alastair can come home tomorrow. I haven't told her about us and I want to,' she said earnestly. 'I want to go home and be a family, Ross.'

Relief crashed through him as he took her in his arms and held her fiercely. Never would he do that again: jump to some stupid conclusion and think ill of her. And how easily he had done that; thought the very worst of her. It said a lot about himself, none of it admirable.

'Of course, darling. We'll leave in the morning,' he earnestly reassured her.

He felt the tension drain out of her as gently he scooped her up into his arms and headed for the bathroom. He set her down and ran the taps and when he turned back to her he saw tears in her eyes. She held out her arms and he went to her again and held her tightly.

'Ross, promise to love me for the rest of our days,' she wept against his neck. 'Promise never to look at another woman. I couldn't bear to lose you after waiting for you for so long.'

His heart broke for her. 'Oh, my darling, don't you know by now how much you mean to me? I'll do anything to make you happy, anything. I hate to see you like this, so dreadfully insecure.'

He kissed her deeply and held her tightly, vowing to cherish her for ever. He fully understood the insecurity inside her but all that was behind her now. Never, ever, would he give her reason to doubt his love.

He left Jenna under a mountain of bubbles, her eyes closed with just the glint of a teardrop on her long lashes. Relaxed and soothed she looked a lot less stressed than before.

As he moved around the galley-type kitchen he wondered what had brought about the sudden change in her today when she had seemed so contented and happy before. He supposed that her mother's news that Alastair was coming home had unsettled her and she wanted to be there for them both. And rightly so.

He broke eggs into a bowl and tossed the shells into a bin under the sink. A piece of crumpled paper which had missed the bin caught his eye and he reached down for it.

A name in the corner of the green advertising pamphlet had him stiffen with horror. He smoothed it out on the stainless steel work surface and beads of sweat broke out on his brow as he read that Marcel DeLuc, was to be a special guest at the opening of an East End art exhibition that very day.

He read it over and over again and then in a fury of disbelief he thrust the offending sheet of paper into the back pocket of his black jeans. Automatically, he tipped salad into a bowl, beat the eggs senseless, cooked the omelettes to within a second of burning and then slumped back against the work surface and pressed his hands to his temples.

It was blindingly obvious; Jenna had been to see Marcel. Why else would that damned piece of paper be here in his apartment? Why should she have gone to that exhibition if it was all over between them? Was the reason for her disturbed state this evening guilt? The pain and the rage of it burned inside him till he could contain it no longer.

'Jenna!' he roared, stepping out of the kitchen into the hallway to cross it and haul Jenna out of the bathroom to explain herself. Then he stopped dead.

'Karen?' he breathed incredulously.

Karen shut the front door behind her and leaned back against it, gazing at him in wide eyed shock. She was dressed for an evening out, in a shiny black trouser suit with a white ruffled blouse and he tried to remember if they'd had an arrangement that had slipped his memory, but his mind was a complete blank.

'How did you get in?' were the first idiotic words that came to his lips.

She gave him a look with the chill of arctic ice. 'I came in the security doors with Patrick from the ground floor apartment and when I got up here your front door wasn't even locked, Ross. I could have been a damned burglar!' She tossed her evening bag on to the hall table and with a furious look of contempt in his direction she strode through to the sitting room.

'Where is she then?' she challenged furiously, swinging round to face him. 'It was her name you were calling when I came in, wasn't it? It certainly didn't sound like, *Karen*!'

'I'm here,' Jenna said from the open doorway. She stood barefoot, dripping puddles onto the golden woodblock floor. She was huddled into his oversize bathrobe, her face flushed as if she had flown out of the bath to find out what was going on.

In spite of that incriminating piece of paper he had found by the bin Ross wanted to gather her up in his arms and get her out of here because he had the strong feeling that Karen was about to cause an unpleasant scene. He remembered Jenna's observation that Karen didn't see their relationship as companionship. Now he realised she was right. Karen wasn't at all pleased to find them here together.

'Karen,' he breathed, 'Jenna and I are spending a few days in town. I'm sorry. It's Friday, isn't it? I should have called.'

'Damn right, you should have called.'

Suddenly she swooped across the room and plunged her index finger down on the answer phone on his desk. To Ross's fevered senses it seemed she had done it for Jenna's benefit, to show that she had an intimate knowledge of his apartment and his life.

'Ross, darling, I'm back from Brussels. My secretary said you'd called. I've tickets for Aida tonight. If you don't call back I'll know you are up for it. I'll pick you up around seven. Can't wait to see you. Cia.'

Ross's frowned worriedly. Had Jenna played that message back and thought the worst, hence her insecurity earlier?

'I'm sorry, Karen. I got stuck in a meeting, came in late and didn't pick up the message.'

'Obviously not,' she snapped, lifted her finger and

pointed it at Jenna. 'But I bet she did if you two have been holed up here together for days. Pleased with yourself, *Jenna*? You're evidently not as innocent as you look. Beware, Ross,' she directed at him. 'She's quite a little schemer. She could have told you about my message but she thought it more fun to let me arrive here to the embarrassment of finding you together in your little love nest.'

Jenna didn't say a word in her own defence but Ross didn't think for a minute that Karen was right. And yet...

Ross followed Karen as she swept into the hallway and snatched up her evening bag.

'Karen, before you leave, let me explain. I called you days ago to tell you about Jenna and me, but you were away. I'm deeply sorry you had to find out this way and I'm deeply sorry that you are taking it so badly. I really didn't think you took our relationship so seriously.'

Karen glared at him. 'No, Ross, I don't suppose you did because you have absolutely no idea of what makes a woman tick. Six months we've been dating and you should have known how I felt about you. You're blind, Ross, more so with that little French tart. She'll tie you in knots until you don't know what hit you. You might be a business whizz, following in your father's footsteps, but you haven't the first idea about women!'

Ross reached for the door and opened it for her. Without a word he closed it after her and stood for a while composing himself. All she had accused him of was true and he regretted hurting her. After Jenna all those years back he had never allowed himself to feel any deep emotions. Selfishly he had never considered

Karen's feelings during their time together.

'Did you hear all that?' Ross said as he joined Jenna in the kitchen. Of course she had but what was surprising was that she wasn't throwing a tantrum. It was obvious he hadn't called Karen to end their relationship as Jenna had asked him to. He'd tried only to find she was away and then...then he'd forgotten about her. It was unforgivable.

She was sliding the cold omelettes into the bin. 'I've been telling you for years,' she murmured. 'You never did understand women.'

Ross pulled a bottle of chilled Chardonnay from the fridge. 'I need a drink,' he growled.

'Me too,' she said softly. 'That wasn't a very nice experience.'

'Nice? That's an understatement. It was appalling and I deserved it.' He uncorked the wine and Jenna held the glasses out. 'So why aren't you jumping down my throat in a rage that I hadn't ended it with Karen before tonight?'

Even as he was speaking the words he knew the answer to that. Jenna had a conscience. She'd been with Marcel this day. All roads led to the fact that she wasn't causing a fuss about Karen because she didn't care enough.

'I'm not stupid, Ross,' she told him after sipping her wine. 'I could work it all out. You called her to tell her about us but she was away. Because she isn't important in your life I suppose you forgot about her. The only sin you've committed is not realising how she truly felt about you.' She sighed deeply and took another sip of wine. 'I'm not mad with you, Ross, but I do feel sorry for Karen. I know from experience that you have difficulty expressing your emotions. It took me years to get you to open up, so what chance did she have after a mere six months?'

She smiled over the rim of her glass. 'I didn't listen to that message as she suggested. It was as much a shock to me as it was to you. And I'm not "a scheming little French tart who will tie you in knots". Her insults fell on deaf ears because I'm adult enough to realise how upset she was.'

The depth of her understanding astounded him. Under normal circumstances he would think how damned lucky he was to have her, but all sensible reasoning had left him after finding out where she had been all day.

'I do love you very much, Ross,' she whispered and leaned up to kiss his chin. She grinned impishly. 'Bring that bottle with you. Let's go to bed and fool around. It's been a funny day.'

As Jenna turned and went through to the sitting room, a red mist swam before Ross's eyes. He felt burning jealousy rip through him in spite of the words she had just spoken. How could she say she loved him when she had deceived him by meeting Marcel behind his back? It hurt like hell but to crown it all the other torment was back when he had thought it had all gone away.

Yvonne was wrong. If Jenna had been told that Marcel carried the same genes as she did, it would have ended it, brutally and finally. Instead she was seeing Marcel again and not even Ross's love and devotion had been able to stop her. He couldn't let it pass.

She sat coiled into the corner of the sofa waiting for him. Ross threw the crumpled piece of evidence down on the glass coffee table in front of her. The smile of expectation faded from her lips and he saw her fingers tighten around the stem of her wine glass.

So his suspicions had a genuine a foundation. Guilt was in her eyes, the set of her mouth and the sudden flush of colour in her cheeks.

'Where did you get that?' she asked in a low voice. Uncoiling her legs she leaned forward to put her wine glass on the table, so nervously that some of it spilled. She didn't touch the pamphlet but stared at it bleakly.

Towering over her Ross told her. 'In the bin where you so carelessly discarded it, Jenna,' he said coldly. 'Pity you didn't have the forethought to discard it elsewhere. But then maybe you intended me to find it? Perhaps to make it a little easier for yourself when you plucked up the courage to tell me that you have decided your heart lies with Marcel after all.'

She said nothing, just stared bleakly at the paper without raising her eyes to his.

'So what was the plan, Jenna? To keep us both on hold while you made up your mind which of us you truly wanted?' he challenged stiffly. 'Did your meeting with Marcel today make it all clear to you?'

She flinched, then shot to her feet and glared at him furiously.

'Why are you so convinced there was a meeting, Ross?' Shakily she pointed at the green pamphlet. 'That could just be junk mail, delivered to the door!'

For an instant he wondered. Junk mail *was* a plague on society. It was possible, but no, his brain suddenly rejected the idea. Jenna wasn't herself tonight. She'd been tense and insecure and then had totally accepted Karen's sudden appearance and swallowed her insults without a qualm. The Jenna of old would have reacted fiercely to such a jibe, but this was a new Jenna, a much more subtle Jenna.

'Deny it then, Jenna,' he challenged darkly. 'Convince me that you weren't at that exhibition today, I'll forget the whole thing and Marcel will never be mentioned again.'

Ross waited. And waited. With her head lowered he couldn't see her eyes but he didn't need to. Her silence was his answer. Then slowly she lifted her face. It was pinched with anguish but he couldn't allow his heart to respond. It was like a rock inside his chest

'Y...yes, I was there,' she admitted helplessly.

Ross's heart did respond then. It shattered into fragments. He'd never felt such pain.

Jenna came around the coffee table and stood in front of him. She looked smaller than ever in his huge bathrobe. Her eyes were wide and smoky as she looked up at him. Tears glistened in their depths. It was a temptation to block it all out and sweep her into his arms but he was made of sterner stuff. He held her eyes censoriously.

'I went to the exhibition,' she started to explain, 'but I didn't know Marcel would be there.'

Ross snapped and let out a cry of exasperation. 'You expect me to believe that! His name is on the programme, isn't it?' He snatched up the paper and waved it in front of her.

Jenna responded by snatching up a copy of the

previous evening's paper from the coffee table. It was folded back to the arts and entertainment's page and she waved it in front of him.

'But it's not in this advert, Ross,' she blazed at him.

Ross read it quickly, his heart thudding dangerously. No mention of Marcel.

'I read about the opening of the exhibition in this paper last night,' she went on. 'I've seen Moyra Lowenstein's work in Paris and I like it very much. She's a sculptress and we met through Marcel, at one of his exhibitions. I had nothing to do, Ross. I'm sick of shopping and sitting around waiting for you to spare me a precious moment of your valuable time...'

'So this is my fault, is it?' he interjected with the accusation. 'You are beginning to sound like your mother!'

'To hell, with you, Ross. Hear me out. I'm not my mother and I never will be. I'm just trying to explain what happened. I went to the exhibition and I was handed the programme at reception. I was shocked to see Marcel's name on it. The steward explained that Marcel was a last minute exhibitor. His name hadn't appeared in the newspaper but they'd had time to have it printed on the handouts.'

Suddenly Jenna slumped down into the sofa and held her head in her hands.

'Oh, Ross, I wish I hadn't gone in,' she sobbed. 'I wish I'd had the strength to walk away but I just couldn't. I had to go in and see him.'

Numbly Ross lowered himself into an armchair across from her. His life blood drained out of him. His worst fears were confirmed. Jenna couldn't let Marcel go. Regardless of the pain he felt inside he had to stop her returning to Marcel but anger erupted before he could tell her the truth.

'You could have walked away from that exhibition without seeing him but you didn't! Have you just been using me these past days, Jenna?' he ground out harshly. 'Whatever was going through your mind? You promised to break off the engagement and you didn't, did you?'

Jenna lifted her tear streaked face. 'But you didn't end it with Karen either!' she blurted.

Ross shot to his feet. 'I'm not listening to any more of this!' he thundered. 'Ten minutes ago you totally accepted my mistake with Karen; very wisely too, I thought. But you had an ulterior motive; you were preparing me for your deception. So what the hell was all that about earlier, that heart rending insecurity ploy; making me promise never to look at another woman? Another of your schemes? Like the one on your eighteenth birthday!'

'You swine!' Jenna threw at him hotly. Shakily she got to her feet and threw the newspaper fiercely at his chest. 'I had a shock today, Ross, and I've been trying to cope with it. True, I didn't break off my engagement with Marcel before today but I tried to. After you left my bedroom that day I called but he wasn't available. But I didn't give up and forget as you did with Karen because I happen to have a heart whereas you haven't. No, I persisted. I've called every day and God knows I've had plenty of opportunity to as you have always been elsewhere.'

She stopped to draw breath, clutching at her throat as

if finding it hard to spit out the words.

'By sheer coincidence I'd picked that exhibition to while away a few hours and Marcel was there. I thought at the time it was fate giving me the chance to break off the engagement in the way I wanted to, face to face. As soon as I entered that hall I realised why Marcel was never available. He was with Moyra, you see. I could see it in their faces as they posed for the press; see it in the way they touched each other. They're an item, Ross, and it looked as if they have been for some time, and I never knew!'

Ross's pulse rate went into overdrive. His throat dried up at the thought she had been so cut up about it that it had torn her world apart.

Pulling her robe tighter around her she lifted her chin bravely as the tears coursed down her face.

'And I know what you are thinking, Ross, but you are wrong,' she cried. 'I'm not jealous or heart broken over Marcel, not one bit, but at that moment of realisation I knew that I had been in danger of making the worst mistake of my life if I had gone through with the marriage. Marcel hadn't changed. He has his father's genes after all. I've no doubt he would have married me because I was "clean". I would have given him respectability while he carried on his affairs behind my back.'

Jenna swallowed hard before going on. 'Marcel saw me and he knew that I knew. I tried to get away but he cornered me, tried out a few feeble lies on me, testing my devotion, testing my weakness but I was strong and told him what he could do with the rest of his life. I've had a lucky escape, Ross, but it doesn't change the fact that I came close to marrying him and making a complete fool of myself.'

'Jenna, darling,' Ross reached for her but she stepped out of his way, knocking the table and sending her wine glass crashing to the floor.

'Don't, Ross. Don't touch me. You've thought the very worst of me tonight and never, never have I done anything to deserve that. I was stressed today because it made me realise what an idiot I had been to think a marriage without love, trust and devotion could ever work. I coped with it though but I was insecure with you tonight because I love you so much that I knew that if you ever let me down I wouldn't be able to cope with it.'

She took another strangled breath. 'But you *have* let me down, Ross. You've ruined my life all over again by not trusting me.'

She turned and stumbled from the room and Ross stood motionless, his head pounding violently. What sort of a fool was he? Couldn't he do one thing right for the woman who had held his heart in her hands for so long? He messed up every time whereas she had it all straight in her mind. Her love had been unwavering. Honest and true. His was distorted with self doubt, pride, every negative feeling imaginable.

So what could he say or do to make it right for her? Whatever, it had to be done. He couldn't lose her again. She was his life

chapter thirteen

Jenna had never known such misery and pain. She stood huddled at Ross's bedroom window gazing out over a sparkling city but seeing nothing but Ross's furious features as he had accused her. How could a man who claimed to love her so deeply mistrust her so badly? Jealousy she could understand but she hadn't given him any reason to feel that way. He had thought the worst without hearing her out and she hadn't deserved that.

If she let this wound inside her fester it would do too much damage and after her long struggle to secure his love she couldn't bear to lose it all over again. But to humble herself in his eyes would only make him believe he could treat her that way again.

She didn't hear the door opening behind her and she jumped nervously as she felt something warm being linked around her neck. Her hand came up and her precious pearl was nestling in the hollow of her throat. Ross lifted her hair and pressed his lips fervently against the clasp, sealing it to her hot skin. Her determination began to weakly slip away and the strength to fight him drained from her.

Closing her eyes tightly she murmured. 'It feels warm.'

'Since you threw it back to me I've kept it in my breast pocket, close to my heart.' he whispered emotionally. 'It's back where it belongs, Jenna.'

Slowly Jenna turned to him and rested her hands on his arms as he held her around her waist. 'And where do I belong, Ross? Outside of your heart? I have done everything in my power to gain your love and I've obviously failed hopelessly.'

He shook his head adamantly. 'The failure is with me and not you, my darling. It's because I love you so desperately and was so afraid of losing you that I allowed demons to rule my thinking and my words. I was so tormented at the thought of you returning to Marcel that I momentarily lost all reasoning. I will never allow it to happen again, Jenna. I promise you that from the bottom of my heart.'

Her eyes filled with tears as she whispered plaintively. 'It should never have crossed your mind in the first place, Ross.' Although she was almost at the point of forgiving him completely there was still a small residue of hurt needing to be soothed away.

'I know that now, but it happened, I did doubt you and my demons are no excuse I know.' He sighed deeply. 'I was so very wrong but if you don't forgive me for the gravest error of my life in misjudging you then we are lost, Jenna. After all we have been through together I couldn't bear to lose you again. I can't even begin to imagine a life without you.'

And if she allowed his demons to dominate her thinking they were indeed lost. He had hurt her badly this night, but if she allowed that hurt to take over she would lose him forever.

Jenna pressed her face into his shoulder and clung to him. 'How can I not forgive you when my life is nothing without you? I do understand how you must have felt and maybe none of this would have happened if I had been honest and told you where I had been today. But I couldn't, Ross. I didn't want to share it with you. It was something I had to deal with on my own. I wanted Marcel out of my life, never to be spoken about or thought about ever again. Complete closure on that part of my life. I just wanted it to be us with no more of the past to get in our way.'

'Jenna, darling,' he whispered into her hair. 'That's what I'm here for, to share everything with you. I don't want you to feel that you can't tell me all that goes on in your head. I hate to think of the day you've had, struggling with so many emotions when I could have helped you.'

She lifted her hand to his cheek and smiled weakly. 'You're right. I should have shared my worries with you and we wouldn't have had this dreadful upset. I want all this pain to go away because it's unbearable. Take me home, Ross,' she pleaded. 'I don't want to be here in town anymore. Bad things have happened here and I want to forget this awful day as soon as I can.'

He kissed her mouth softly and tenderly and at last Jenna felt the black clouds move away leaving her free of all anxiety. Neither of them would ever let this sort of mistrust affect them again, of that she was sure. Their love was too deep and too strong.

They left the Knightsbridge apartment half an hour later. While Ross had sorted and packed some paperwork away in his briefcase Jenna moved silently and methodically around the rooms. She wiped Karen's message from the answering machine, she binned the newspaper and the green pamphlet and swept up her broken wine glass. She felt as if she was cleaning her mind of all reminders of their past without each other. It would just be the two of them from now on.

Two hours later as the car tyres crunched up the driveway of Amersham Hall Jenna smiled contentedly to herself in the darkness. This time the Hall would deliver what it had promised so long ago. She was home at last, with the wonderful man she was going to spend the rest of her life with, and nothing would ever come between them again. She reached out for Ross's hand and he squeezed hers tightly as if he knew just what she was thinking.

'Surely you can do better than that, Jenna,' Alastair laughed as Jenna gave him a hesitant hug of welcome in the hallway.

Ross had driven to the hospital to pick his father and her mother up and Jenna had stayed behind with Charlotte to make sure everything was just perfect for his homecoming.

With a laugh Jenna gave him a bear hug. 'I was afraid I might hurt you.'

'I haven't broken any bones. I had a ridiculous heart attack that's all.' He held her at arm's length. 'Let me have a proper look at you.'

'You saw me at the hospital the first day,' Jenna protested lightly, blushing slightly as Alastair looked her up and down approvingly.

'I was so doped up I couldn't see a hand in front of my face,' he chuckled. 'You look wonderful, Jenna, my dear. I can see Ross has been spoiling you in London.'

Jenna grinned at Ross behind his father's back.

'You know,' Alastair mused as he gazed around the hall at the flowers Jenna had carefully arranged for him, 'I never thought I'd see this place again.'

'Stop that this minute, Alastair,' Yvonne cajoled quickly; instantly at his side and taking his arm to steer him gently towards the stairway.

'Huh, if you think I'm going up to bed at four o'clock in the afternoon, you are very much mistaken,' Alastair said firmly as he steered Yvonne towards the drawing room. 'I need a drink. We all need a drink,' he insisted.

'Is that wise?' Yvonne fussed with a frown of concern as they all walked through to the drawing room.

'Wise or not I'm having a small whisky to get the taste of the hospital out of my mouth. Don't fuss Yvonne, I asked permission of the consultant before I left. In moderation it won't kill me.'

'Don't talk like that, Alastair. You know it upsets me. Well I insist you take it with a litre of water at the very least. Oh, Ross, you've lit a fire for us,' Yvonne enthused, stepping towards the flaming logs with her hands outstretched. 'How thoughtful of you.'

'Jenna lit it actually,' Ross volunteered as he went to the drinks cabinet. 'She remembered how you loved the open fires here in England.'

Yvonne glanced at Jenna as if suddenly remembering she had a daughter. Jenna wasn't unduly surprised. She guessed her mother was feeling guilty for the lies she had told about Ross loving her and wanting to marry her. When she had called the London apartment to say that Alastair was coming home Jenna had had the feeling she had expected to speak to Ross and not her.

Yvonne hadn't mentioned their last phone call when she had put the phone down on her and Jenna certainly hadn't wanted to. Everything still needed to be ironed out between them, but not now. Now was all about Alastair's homecoming.

Yvonne stepped towards Jenna to give her a small hug. 'Thank you, darling, that was sweet of you.'

She stepped back quickly and Jenna's heart sank a little. It was just like Paris when her mother could barely bring herself to speak to her. She so wanted to put her mother's mind at rest about Marcel, and to tell her that she had been right all along, he was and always had been thoroughly unsuitable marriage material. And of course to impart the wonderful news that she and Ross were going to be married. But wisely Ross had advised her to wait till Alastair was settled back into his routine before they told everyone.

'I'll go and see if everything is all right with Charlotte in the kitchen,' Jenna said quickly.

'That's not your place to, Jenna,' Yvonne said abruptly. 'I'm here now and can handle everything.'

Jenna stiffened but said nothing at the rebuke, which no one else seemed to have noticed. It seemed her mother was indeed back and taking control and who was she to argue.

Yvonne leaned over the tapestry wing chair by the fireplace where Alastair sat nursing the small whisky and water Ross had just poured him and kissed the top of his head. 'I called Charlotte earlier to bring the evening meal forward by an hour, darling. In future we'll eat at six instead of seven as before. And no more red meat, it's not good for you. Chicken this evening.'

At the door she turned. 'No more of that whisky for your father, Ross. One is quite enough.'

As she closed the door quietly behind her Alastair held the glass up to Ross in a silent request. Ross responded by defiantly adding another short measure of whisky with a good splash of water. They exchanged a conspiratorial smile.

'Honestly, you two,' Jenna laughed as she flopped onto the sofa. Ross handed her a glass of white wine accompanied by a smile of adoration for her eyes only.

'I know what you two must be thinking,' Alastair laughed, 'but let it be. Yvonne's sudden exertion of authority is born out of concern for my health. Poor darling has been through hell lately.' He turned his head towards Jenna and Jenna prayed he wasn't going to bring up her engagement to Marcel as a further reason for her mother's hell.

'I don't know if your mother has told you but she's not going back to Paris.'

'No, she hasn't but I suspected as much,' Jenna replied.

'Well I'm sure she'll get around to having a heart to heart with you before long. We've both done a lot of soul searching at the hospital. Your mother never left my side you know. We were foolish to let our marriage slip through our fingers.' He shrugged. 'We're reunited now and things are going to change. I shall retire of course and devote all my time to my wife. How do you feel about that, Ross?' he asked with a hint of concern.

Ross, leaning against the marble mantelpiece with a glass in his hand smiled down at his father. 'How could

I object when I've been trying to get you to ease up myself?'

'It means more pressure on you, I'm afraid. I've a feeling Karen won't take too kindly to that. You know what women are like. She sent me flowers and a card, you know. Said she hopes to see me very soon. You'll have to invite her down one weekend...'

Shakily Jenna got to her feet, not wishing to hear any more. She gave Ross an agonised look and his eyes appeared so desolate that his father had brought Karen's name into the conversation that she felt remorse for looking at him that way. She smiled quickly and shrugged her shoulders at him. She'd dealt with her doubts and knew that Ross was hers and not Karen's but it troubled her that Alastair didn't know.

Ross caught her in the hallway on the way to the kitchen. 'I'm sorry about that,' he said quickly.

Jenna gripped his arms and smiled warmly. 'It's OK. Your father wasn't to know. Oh, Ross, already this is getting awkward. Alastair thinks you are still with Karen and...' her eyes sparkled and she lowered her voice. 'I don't want to have to move back into my own bedroom and I'll have to if we keep this to ourselves for much longer.'

Ross laughed and hugged her. 'This house is big enough for me to run a harem without anyone noticing.'

'You wouldn't dare!'

'I wouldn't want to,' he growled at her affectionately.

Jenna widened her eyes. 'I don't know how long I can keep this quiet,' she said with concern. 'Didn't you notice how my mother is with me? She obviously still thinks I'm going ahead with my wedding plans. Did she say anything about it at the hospital when you arrived to pick them up?

'We were with Alastair all the time. She wouldn't say anything in front of him. She didn't even mention London or you come to that.'

'Evidently still burying her head in the sand where I'm concerned,' Jenna huffed. 'It's as if I don't exist in her world.'

'She's probably feeling guilty for what she told you about me loving you and wanting to marry you and more than likely embarrassed about the whole business,' Ross reasoned.

'I did think that myself,' Jenna admitted. 'And of course she has no idea about us. Well if she is feeling that way I need to talk to her about it and clear the air. She can't go on cutting me dead now that we are all together in the house.'

'She's not cutting you dead, Jenna. She's simply a bit uncomfortable with you. Don't forget you've been like this for weeks now, arguing over this marriage of yours. She's been through a lot and is still rather wrapped up with my father at the moment. It's his first night home and...'

He stopped at the sight of her crinkling her nose at all he was saying. 'You don't want to wait any longer, do you?'

Jenna shook her head. 'I understand your thinking, Ross, I really do and we needn't tell Alastair right away if you would prefer it that way, but this thing with my mother is only going to get worse if I don't tell her that I'm going to marry you and not Marcel. I hate having it hanging over us all like this. I want my mother back, to wipe the slate clean and for us all to start being a proper family.'

At last Ross nodded his head. 'You're right. Yvonne needs to be put out of her misery and so do you. As far as my father is concerned, well, I guess it would do his heart more good than harm to tell him as well.' He grinned at her. 'If your mother is anything like you she won't be able to contain herself anyway.'

Jenna squealed with excitement that Ross didn't want to delay their news any longer than she did. She flung her arms around him and half squeezed him to death. 'Oh, Ross, every minute of my life gets better and better with you.'

Ross smoothed a hand down the side of her face. 'I love you, Jenna Cameron,' he said softly.

She raised her lips to his. 'I'm not a Cameron yet but already I love the sound of it. We'll tell them tonight over dinner. Ross. I'm so relieved and happy. ' She kissed him deeply and lovingly and when she drew back from him her eyes were dancing as she said suggestively. 'I bought a new dress in London for just this occasion. Do you want to come upstairs and take your time zipping me into it?'

Ross smiled in submission but caught her hand as she swung towards the stairs.

'It's not burgundy silk dripping in oyster pearl beads, is it?' he teased.

Jenna burst out laughing. 'No way. This one isn't a cry for help. This one says, come and get me I'm all yours!' With that she flew up the stairs, two at a time.

'You weren't fooling, were you?' Ross laughed when Jenna whipped the gorgeous sleek bright red creation out of his wardrobe to hold it up against her. He frowned suddenly. 'It reminds me of something.'

'Yes, a certain red satin mini dress,' she told him breathlessly. 'The one I wore on my eighteenth birthday.' She stepped towards him and went on softly. 'But this one is different, Ross. It's a little bit longer, ' she laughed, 'and it covers my cleavage, a little bit more, and it's silk and not satin. It's far more mature and sophisticated and sensible. Just like me.'

Ross laughed and snatched at the dress and tossed it carelessly on the floor. He pulled her hard against him, aroused and hungry for her.

'Whatever you say about it, it's having the same fate as the birthday dress. And so are you!' he muttered into her ear before pushing her back on the bed and falling across her.

chapter fourteen

'Are you sure you're ready for this?' Ross asked Jenna as hand in hand they came down the stairs later. The grandfather clock chimed six as they reached the bottom step. 'It's going to be quite a shock for them.'

'A pleasant one though,' Jenna said hopefully. 'I'm nervous all the same. I shall probably be a wreck on my wedding day. How does this dress suit me, Ross?' she asked as they crossed the hallway to the open doors of the drawing room.

'You sounded just like Paloma then,' Ross laughed, remembering Jenna's Spanish girlfriend.

'I must call her soon and tell her the news. Are you sure I look OK?'

'I keep telling you, you looking ravishing.'

'You said ravished upstairs,' she teased.

'I think the word I used was impoverished after seeing the price tag.'

They were both laughing as they stepped into the drawing room.

'Oh, there's no one here,' Jenna said with disappointment as she gazed around at the empty room.

Ross frowned. It wasn't like his father to be a minute late for anyone or anything. He considered unpunctuality bad manners. But then Ross remembered that everyone's lives had changed lately. In a way he hoped his father was late down to dinner. It would prove that his intentions to take things easy were sincere.

'Perhaps Yvonne has forgotten the routine. Drinks here before adjourning to the dining room.' He reached down to pack a large oak log on to the hot embers of the fire.

'Or perhaps they are busy making up for lost time,' Jenna suggested as she sat on the sofa and kicked off her high heels.

Ross looked at her, startled. The thought had never crossed his mind.

'Don't look so appalled, Ross,' Jenna laughed. 'They've both been married three times. I'm sure they know what it's all about by now.'

Twice only, in Yvonne's case Ross mused as he poured walked towards her. But Jenna would never know that. He was glad that at last it was all over with. He was infinitely grateful he had never told Jenna the truth and in one way it was good that Jenna had found out for herself what sort of a person Marcel was. Seeing him with another woman was security for the future. She'd never want to see him again and that was the way it should be.

'I've persuaded Alastair not to come down for dinner,' Yvonne stated as she swept into the room in an elegant olive green silk dress with pearls at her throat. 'He's had quite enough excitement for one day.'

Ross caught Jenna's dancing eyes and she was giving him a look of I told you so. Smiling, he shook his head and poured a sherry for Yvonne as she stood in front of the fire warming herself.

'Thank you, Ross.' She took the glass but didn't lift

it to her lips. 'Before I take his dinner up to him I have something to tell you both. I expect you can guess what it is but I'd like to announce it formally all the same.' She paused to smile happily at them in turn and then she raised her glass. 'Alastair and I are reconciled. I'm sure you'd like to join me in a toast to our future happiness.'

Ross watched Jenna as her face brightened as if the news was a surprise to her. Not to spoil Yvonne's excitement by saying they already knew Ross too, faked surprise.

'It's wonderful news, Yvonne,' he said enthusiastically and leaned across the fireplace to kiss her on the cheek.

Yvonne said quickly, putting her glass down on the coffee table. 'I need to see Charlotte about Alastair's supper Ross, but I'll join you for dinner of course.'

Jenna quickly got to her feet.

'Don't go yet, Mamma.' She put her arms around her mother and hugged her tightly. 'I'm so pleased for you and Alastair,' she said sincerely, her eyes bright with happiness. She stepped back from her to take her hands. 'Ross and I are delighted for you both. We're thrilled that you are back together again.'

'Yes, it's wonderful news, Yvonne,' Ross repeated warmly but was rather perturbed to see Yvonne lower her head and draw her hands out from her daughters.

'Yes, well there is only one thing marring my happiness, Jenna,' she said rather stiffly and pointedly. She went to turn away from her daughter.

Jenna caught her mother's arm. 'Don't keep turning your back on me, Mamma,' she said plaintively.

Stealing a glance at Ross she seemed to be asking permission to go on.

Ross nodded. Now was exactly the time to reveal all. This tension between mother and daughter couldn't go on any longer.

Jenna took a deep breath and spoke softly. 'I know what is troubling you, Mamma, and I have some news for you too. I'm not going to marry Marcel.'

The relief on Yvonne's face warmed Ross through to the bone. Her features suddenly glowed with such happiness that Ross himself was relieved it was all over.

'Oh, Jenna,' she cried, falling into her daughters arms. 'I can't tell you how happy I am. This has all been such a strain for me and I've been so awful with you. Forgive me, darling.'

'I know, Mamma, I know what you've been through,' Jenna soothed, stroking her back. 'And I'm not cross or bitter with you anymore for asking Ross to intervene to stop my wedding. I realise you were so desperate you couldn't cope on your own. The marriage would have been morally wrong and you knew that but you weren't strong enough to confide in me.'

'M...morally wrong!' Yvonne suddenly cried, and wrenched herself out of Jenna's arms.

Ross stood as if paralysed, his grip on the crystal decanter so hard he was in danger of snapping the neck off. His whole insides were constricted into a knot as those two words reverberated in his head. Ross knew what Jenna meant; morally wrong in the sense that she had considered marriage to a man she didn't love but Yvonne had an entirely different take on the words.

Jenna had spoken in innocence but her mother hadn't heard it that way.

Yvonne swung on Ross, no longer the happy relieved mother but a tortured soul once again. Her face was suddenly pinched and her eyes narrowed and distraught.

'Yvonne, don't!' he warned thickly, sensing what was coming.

His impassioned plea went unheard as she screamed at him hysterically.

'You've told her, Ross! You promised me you wouldn't tell her but you couldn't swallow your disgust, could you? Is this your revenge for what you think I am? For what I did all those years ago! I wanted to protect Jenna from all of this. I never wanted her to know about her father.'

'Mamma!' Jenna cried in confusion.

'Stop this, Yvonne!' Ross ordered sharply this time.

But his order went unheeded as Yvonne lunged towards him in a fury. Ross caught her hands and held them firmly. Restrained from making a physical attack Yvonne spat more vitriol at him.

'Don't you think I have suffered enough knowing Jenna wanted to marry her half brother? No, you have to add more misery by insisting on the damned truth. You had no right to do that!'

'Stop it! Stop it!' Jenna screamed.

Yvonne froze. Ross froze.

'Oh, my God, Oh, my God,' Jenna was repeating, dazed and shocked, her white face twisted with pain.

Thrusting Yvonne aside Ross went to her. 'Jenna, darling.'

'Don't touch me!' she hissed, backing away from him. 'Don't anyone come near me! Just tell me this isn't happening. Tell me I misunderstood!' Her eyes flicked from her mother to Ross, pleading with them both to tell her that she had.

Yvonne let out a ragged moan of realisation and groaned helplessly. 'Oh, what have I done?' She looked at Ross, her eyes brimming with pain. 'You didn't tell her, did you?' she rasped.

'No, I didn't tell her,' Ross whispered and turned his attention to Jenna who was swaying with shock.

'Jenna, it's true. Gerard is your real father and Marcel's your half brother,' he told her softly and reached out for her, but she was already backing away from him again. He stopped; too afraid to pursue her in case she completely crumbled.

Her pinched mouth formed a tremulous repetition of his words. 'G...Gerard my father? M...Marcel is...is my half brother? Suddenly her fearful eyes hardened. 'And you knew?' she accused Ross.

'Yes, I did know, Jenna,' Ross admitted. They were past the point of anyone coming out of this unscathed. The truth was out and had to be faced but he knew the suffering Jenna was going through. He was desperate to help her but feeling hopelessly powerless. Whatever words were spoken, nothing would ease the hurt for her at this moment.

She shook her head in disbelief and turned to her mother. 'All those years I asked you about my real father,' she cried heatedly. 'You couldn't tell me then and you never did. You didn't even have the courage to tell me why you wanted to stop my wedding. You just left me floundering. I will never forgive you for this, Mamma, *never*!'

In a rage she faced Ross. 'And I will never forgive you for this either, Ross,' she flamed. 'I really believed that you loved me but you don't. You were simply acting under orders. *Her* orders,' she nodded contemptuously at her mother. *'Marry her yourself and stop her marrying her brother.'*

'Jenna, no, that isn't true,' Yvonne insisted, her face as ashen and anguished as her daughter's. 'I never gave any orders. I just asked for his help. '

'And he gave it, Mamma,' she seethed through tight lips. 'He stopped me marrying Marcel by proposing to me himself.'

'Oh, Ross! 'Yvonne sobbed.

'I proposed to you because I love you, Jenna,' Ross told her firmly. 'Yvonne, I'd like you to leave us now. Jenna and I need to talk.'

'Save your breath, Ross! Nothing you ever say again will make any difference,' Jenna cried hotly, tears pouring down her cheeks. 'You have wickedly deceived me. You promised to marry me to cover all this up, to protect her, to protect your father, to protect *yourself* from this...this shameful scandal!'

'Jenna, nothing is going to be achieved by hysterics...'

'I have a *right* to hysterics!' Jenna sobbed, shaking from head to toe. 'You all knew but chose to keep it from me. I was planning to marry my own blood but not one of you thought that was a serious enough reason to stop me. Not one of you had the courage to do right by me. I hate you all for that. I will never,

ever forgive any of you!'

Jenna turned and stumbled towards the door, staggering against furniture. In a fury she pulled at the doors and flew out of the room.

Yvonne went to go after her but Ross restrained her.

'Leave it for a while, Yvonne,' he said quietly.

'I have to go to her, Ross,' Yvonne pleaded. 'Everything she said is...is so right. I've done so much wrong and I need to...'

'You were only trying to protect her, Yvonne'

Ross was calm now and needed to be for everyone's sake. It had happened. The terrible truth had come out in the worst possible way but from now on it needed to be handled sensitively. Jenna needed to be alone for a while because there was no chance of reasoning with her now.

Yvonne collapsed on to the sofa, her hands over her face, her sobs of distress so heart-rending Ross went to her and put his arm around her shoulder to comfort her. It was in his heart to forgive her everything because her suffering too was immeasurable. She had carried the weight of her youthful mistake for so long, so deeply that she had never been able to reason that Jenna should have known from the start. He too was as guilty. Blindly he had thought the truth need never be known once he had won her heart.

'I'm equally to blame, Yvonne,' Ross admitted. 'I should have insisted on the truth when you first told me.'

Yvonne nodded and lifted her head. 'You did, Ross. I was the one who didn't want Jenna to know of her heritage. For my own selfish reasons. Shame and pride,' she whispered fretfully. 'And you put me to shame, Ross, willing to marry her to save her?'

Ross shook his head. 'No, not for that reason. I meant what I said to her just now. I want to marry her because I love her with all my heart.'

Yvonne let out a small laugh through her tears. 'You didn't fool Jenna and you don't fool me, Ross. You two were never friends. You hadn't seen her for three years. A few days in London and suddenly you are madly in love? I can't believe that.'

Sighing heavily Ross got up and poured himself a stiff whisky. 'It started years ago, Yvonne,' he told her. 'I'll spare you the details but it's enough to say that we've been in each others hearts for a very long time. When you summoned me to Paris to stop her wedding I realised that we'd punished each other enough. It progressed from there.'

Eyes widened, Yvonne stared at him in disbelief. Ross swallowed his whisky in one gulp trying to take away the despairing thought that if he hadn't allowed Jenna to walk out on him after her birthday, none of this would be happening now.

'Just like old times,' Alastair chuckled as he walked into the room. 'Jenna slamming around. She nearly took the hinges off her bedroom door. It's good to be home.'

Yvonne shot to her feet. 'Alastair…'

Raising his palm to still her before she started, he came towards the fire. 'I'm not staying upstairs like an invalid. Plenty of time for that when I'm really old,' he laughed as he sat down in his fireside chair. 'And no, I'm not having a drink so don't look at me that way,

Yvonne.' He stopped suddenly and looked from his wife to his son with concern. 'Why so serious, you two?'

Ross put down his empty glass and decided that his father was strong enough to hear of the latest developments. Providing Yvonne was strong enough not to collapse into a heap they could all get through this together.

'I've just told Yvonne some rather surprising news, father,' Ross began. He smiled at Yvonne in a way that said it was going to be all right. She looked at him hesitantly but then in resignation she nodded and sank down to the edge of the sofa, clasping her hands tightly together in her lap.

'Well go on, don't keep me in suspense,' Alastair urged.

'The reason that Yvonne is looking so serious is that she can't quite believe that I have loved her daughter for so long,' Ross started. 'We are going to be married, father.'

'You and Jenna! I can't believe it, son!' Alastair laughed incredulously. 'But how on earth did all this come about? I'm delighted of course but only last week you were adamant that she meant nothing to you. You didn't want to go to Paris and...'

'She's everything in my life,' Ross interrupted quietly but fervently. 'But as you once told me, we are all allowed one mistake in our lives. Now remember those words, father. They are very relevant to what Yvonne is going to tell, after I leave you to go to Jenna.' Ross paused to glance at Yvonne. She was subdued, with the fight gone out of her. Ross went on.

'We are very alike, Father, you and I; the mirror image of each other if we did but know it. You allowed Yvonne to walk out on you and did nothing to stop her because of your foolish pride.'

Alastair nodded in agreement but looked slightly confused all the same.

'I allowed Jenna to do the very same thing to me. We were lovers when she was eighteen,' he confessed.

Yvonne gasped and his father's eyes widened but Ross went on. 'I let her walk away from me because of that very same pride, but it was the biggest mistake of my life, the one we are all allowed. Fate has brought you and Yvonne back together again and that same fate has brought Jenna and me together and I know in my heart that neither of us will ever want to experience that separation again.'

Alastair nodded and looked at Yvonne. Tears filled her eyes and slowly she got up and went to him. She knelt at his feet and took one of his hands and pressed it to her lips.

'I have so much to tell you, Alastair,' she said softly. 'If you have half the understanding of Ross I know you will forgive me.'

Looking more confused than ever Alastair glanced at his son.

Ross smiled and leaned down to kiss the top of Yvonne's head. Yvonne took his hand and squeezed it tightly.

'Ross, tell my daughter that I love her very much. I intend to tell her myself of course but this isn't easily resolved, is it?'

'When is anything easily resolved with Jenna?'

he smiled.

'Will someone tell me what is going on here!' Alastair asked in despair.

'I'll leave you now,' Ross breathed. To Yvonne he said, 'You have nothing to worry about, you never did have where my father is concerned. His heart is in the right place, so to speak.'

Ross closed the drawing room doors after him and leaned back against them and closed his eyes. He was drained, right down to his bones. The soft murmur of voices behind him was confirmation that all would be well between his father and Yvonne. He'd never had any doubts in his mind that his father would act with anything other than complete understanding and now Yvonne realised that too.

It was one hurdle successfully accomplished but the rest stretched out before him like an unendurable slog to the winning post — Jenna.

The shock and the horror of her discovery was planted deeply in his heart. Hurting him as much as it was hurting her.

'Mr Cameron, are you all right?' Charlotte asked with concern. 'I'm getting a bit worried about supper. It will spoil if I keep it warm much longer.'

Ross came back to the present with a jolt.

'Keep it warm a little longer if you would, Charlotte.' He forced a smile. 'Maybe someone will feel like eating later.'

But not himself, or Jenna, Ross thought as he strode across the hall to the stairs. He had a long night ahead of him. Another heartbreakingly difficult one. Jenna had proved her ability to rationalise, understand and forgive but all that maturity had disappeared with her devastating discovery. She was back in her troubled past, propelled there by what she now knew. And none of it had been her own doing.

Only a short while ago she had been so blissfully happy and now she was back in her emotional hell; an insecure child again. It was up to him to drag her back again and convince her that his love for her came straight from his heart.

He wasn't going to give up on her and he wouldn't allow her to give up on herself. They had a life to lead together. This wasn't the end of her world but the beginning *of their world*.

chapter fifteen

Jenna lay on the top of her bed, dry-eyed at last, a pillow held against her stomach for comfort. She'd worked it all out in her head and everything added up and the final analysis was too awful to contemplate. She felt pain and anger and disbelief.

Ever since she could remember she had begged her mother to tell her who her father was. And now she knew but there was no comfort or even relief in the knowledge. Just a dreadful, dreadful despairing sickness inside her. She had met him, once. Too busy to look at her properly Gerard had merely shaken her hand politely and turned away. She had touched her own father and never known.

And Marcel...Jenna sat up quickly and pulled the pillow into her stomach more tightly to stop the wave of nausea that cramped her insides. Closing her eyes she tried to block out his image, so many images of him, but it was impossible. Her half brother. The man she had wanted to marry to put the past behind her and start afresh! Thank God their relationship had never progressed beyond a few chaste kisses.

'Oh, God,' she moaned. How could her mother have let it go on? It had been wickedly cruel and never would she forgive Yvonne for her selfish weakness,

But what was worse was Ross's involvement. He had known and hadn't told her. He'd just sent her mind crazy with his declarations of love when all the time it was phoney; all put on to make her break her engagement and save her from marrying the one man she wasn't allowed to marry.

It was unbearable, a betrayal of *her* love that she would never get over. She had given him her all, her heart, her soul, her life. He'd given her nothing but a false declaration of his love and that was as wickedly cruel as what her had mother had done to her.

She heard a light tap at her bedroom door and Ross called out softly. 'Jenna.' Jenna leapt from the bed and quickly turned the key in the lock before he could get in.

'Jenna, don't lock me out,' he moaned, twisting the door knob but to no avail.

Jenna leaned her cheek against the bare wood and closed her eyes tightly.

'I can't talk, Ross,' she whispered hoarsely.

'Darling, I want to share this with you, just as we promised each other in London. You can't manage this on your own.'

'I have to Ross,' she groaned helplessly. 'It...it's too much to share. It's about me and not us anymore.'

'It is about us, Jenna,' Ross insisted. 'You have enough to cope with without believing that I only wanted to marry you to save you marrying Marcel. I want to convince you that it isn't so and then I want to hear what you are going through. You have been dealt a severe blow and we have to talk it through.'

'Please, Ross,' Jenna implored, her wide-spread fingers pressing hard against the door. 'I...I can't face you or anyone else. I beg of you to leave me alone.'

She heard his fists pound frustratedly on the other side of the door and then silence. Slowly Jenna slid down the door and sat coiled in a heap on the floor. She leant her aching head against the panelling and breathed raggedly. She couldn't face him and perhaps tomorrow she couldn't either, but she wouldn't know how she felt till the dawn came.

At last she got up and shakily went to her bathroom. She took a long, long shower, feeling unclean as if she had in fact given herself to Marcel. Exhausted she crawled into bed only to stare blindly up at the ceiling as the moon waxed and waned.

She awoke to a bright sunny day but her heart was still leaden and her head thick with grief. She blinked open her eyes and Ross was sitting on the edge of her bed watching her.

'Spare key,' he said before she asked.

'It took you all night to find it, did it?' she snarled sarcastically as she sat up, pulling her comfort duvet up around her chin. The pain hadn't eased during the interminable night and the sight of him looking at her as if he actually cared didn't help either. She was destined for this pit of misery for the rest of her life.

'I knew where it was but I thought you needed space and solitude. Did you manage to sleep?'

Her eyes went skywards. 'Oh, yes, like a log. Best night's sleep of my life!'

'Jenna, my love, sarcasm doesn't help.'

'It was a silly question, Ross,' she huffed.

He nodded. 'Yes it was and I expect a lot more silly things are going to be said before this is over.'

'It never will be over, Ross, don't you see that?' she

implored. 'I'm seriously damaged inside; so badly my life will never be the same again. The pain will never go away. Nothing you or anyone else can say will make any difference.'

'Then you are a lost soul,' he murmured with a shrug, as if that was it and nothing more need be said on the subject. 'Would you like coffee or juice? I made you some toast too if you can manage it.' He got up from the bed and went to a tray on the dressing table.

Jenna closed her eyes and leant her head on her knees. Yes, she was a lost soul.

She lifted her head and took the glass of orange juice he was holding out to her. She thought he was going to leave her in her misery but he didn't. He sat on the edge of the bed again.

'Don't you want to hear the whole story before you give up completely?' he asked. He reached for her hand but she clasped them both around her glass and sipped the juice without looking at him.

'Nothing you can add will make me feel any better. I've had the whole night to piece everything together.' She sighed deeply. 'I knew my mother was only eighteen when she gave birth to me: a student. When I was little I used to imagine that my father was a professor at her university, older than her of course, but they were besotted with each other. I imagined a terrible tragedy in which he died and my mother was so grief stricken she couldn't ever talk about it. But at least she had me and I was the most important person in her life because I was a part of him. Now I know differently.'

She smiled ruefully, but her words were bitingly cryptic. 'She wasn't married and it was all fantasy in my childish mind. I was the bastard product of a sordid affair with a married man who already had a son of his own. My mother broke up that marriage. I remembered your expression when I was telling you about Marcel's ring. You knew.'

Ross shook his head. 'Your mother didn't know he was married at the time, Jenna. This is part of the problem. When she found out she was so deeply ashamed she buried it all inside her. I don't think she was even aware she had broken up the marriage. She never mentioned it to me but if she did know, it would have given her more guilt to carry. Jenna, she kept quiet to protect you,' he tried to reason. 'Can't you begin to understand the torment she has carried all those years?'

Jenna narrowed her eyes. 'No, I can't, Ross, I can't. She didn't keep quiet to protect me, she only wanted to protect herself from scandal! She's selfish!'

Ross's eyes hardened. 'If she was, Jenna, she would never have given birth to you in the first place.'

Jenna flinched, her fingers tightening around the glass. Her eyes widened painfully. 'W...what do you mean?' she asked faintly.

'Think about it, Jenna,' Ross reasoned calmly. 'She found herself pregnant; a young student with no one to turn to. Her parents were dead and she had inherited wealth to carry her through life. It would have been the easiest thing in the world for her to have an abortion. But she didn't. She wanted you. She'd made a mistake but she was determined you weren't going to pay for it.'

Jenna's head spun for a few blinding seconds and then her mind steadied and her eyes widened painfully.

'I hear you, Ross, 'she uttered hopelessly,' and...and I understand but don't you see? I'm paying for it *now*!'

Suddenly she felt the anger bubbling up inside her. True, her mother had always done what she thought best for her. Though Jenna had rebelled against that many times, she was old enough now to realise that her mother had always had the best intentions for her.

'Just when I needed her most she let me down, Ross,' she blurted heatedly, tossing aside her empty glass and kicking out of her bed covers. Furiously she pulled on her robe and glared down at Ross who was sitting stiffly on her bed.

'When I told my mother I was going to marry Marcel DeLuc she should have told me then. But she didn't. She did nothing to stop it, nothing! For all she knew we could have been sleeping together...sleeping with my own...'

Ross shot to his feet, and grasped her firmly by her arms. 'If she thought that she would have told you, Jenna. From what I gather you told her you weren't sleeping with him. She believed you were still a virgin. It was the one thing that kept her sane till she could think of some way to stop your wedding without having to tell you the awful truth. It's why she sent for me. In her desperation for a solution to save you from hell, she sent for me.'

Wrenching herself away from him Jenna cried. 'But you brought your own brand of hell, Ross. You were willing to marry me to save me from the other hell and whatever you say you can't change the feeling of betrayal I carry. After all this how can I have faith in anything you say again?'

'We've been through this before, Jenna, it's well trodden ground which we have already covered. I love you and want to marry you. Not to save you from your past but because I want us to have a future together.'

'That's impossible now, Ross,' she breathed angrily. 'It's spoiled, ruined. My mother has shifted her guilt and shame on to me. I carry the burden now and I carry it alone. I shall drag it out with me when I leave this house. Between you, you have destroyed any hope of happiness I might have had.'

'So you are throwing away what we have to punish your mother for her mistakes?' Ross raged at her.

'To punish you *both* for deceiving me, Ross.'

'You're punishing yourself, Jenna. You can't make your mother suffer any more than she is already. And you can't punish me because I'm not up for it.'

'Yes, because your heart was never in it in the first place!' Jenna argued. Her eyes warred with his. 'You did all of this out of pity and to protect the Cameron name because we are all involved. I'm damned if I can live with that!'

Ross looked deeply into her eyes, then he shrugged helplessly and held his palms up in submission. His words chilled Jenna to her very marrow.

'Pity never came into it, Jenna. But what's the point of arguing with you any more? Pack your bags and run again. If you are so determined to end it then so be it. I've tried to convince you that you are surrounded by love here but you won't listen. You want to suffer so who am I to stand in your way? Go.'

Tears sprang to Jenna's eyes but she swallowed hard.

Licking her dry lips she uttered weakly. 'You're trying to do it again, aren't you?'

Ross raised a dark brow questioningly.

'You're saying the opposite of what you mean to make me stay. Well it won't work this time.'

Ross gave her a thin smile. 'If I remember rightly it didn't work last time.' He shook his head. 'You're wrong, Jenna. I want you to go.' He reached for her and took her by her shoulders. His touch was tender and Jenna's body stiffened. He bent his head and brushed his lips gently against hers and then looked deep into her eyes.

'I love you so much I can't bear you to stay,' he whispered softly. 'I realise now that you don't love me at all. If you did you wouldn't try to punish me this way. I want you to leave, Jenna, because every time I look at you, you are a reminder of my failure.' He smiled thinly and ran the backs of his fingers down the side of her cheek. 'You know I don't take kindly to failure.'

Jenna's heart thudded helplessly. This was cruel and so unfair. Her brain was on overload and now this, *his* rejection of *her*. It was like a physical slap in the face and it brought her round. It wasn't *his* failure it was all hers. So deeply shocked at what she now knew, she had turned her fury on the one person who mattered more to her than her own life. She swallowed hard, her throat so dry it ached. She tried to say all the words that were suddenly crowding her lips but...but it was too late.

Ross stepped back from her. 'Goodbye, Jenna,' he finalised.

He was gone before she could stop him, so coldly and determinedly she felt real fear in her heart.

Do you need a push?'

Jenna grated her heels on the damp grass to stop her motion on the old swing. So deep was she sunk into her miserable thoughts that she hadn't heard Alastair approach.

Resting her head on the worn rope she watched him lean back against the trunk of the huge old oak tree, and plunge his hands into the pockets of his Barbour jacket as the sun was going down and the temperature with it.

'Shouldn't you be resting, Alastair?' she suggested caringly. Her conscience pricked that he must have come to look for her.

He laughed softly. 'You sound like your mother. She thinks I'm resting now but I sneaked out. Promise you won't tell.'

'I won't,' she laughed.

He sighed deeply. 'This was where I told Ross his mother had died. The nanny had brought him down here to the swing. He was barely four and I went through the usual stuff, mummy's gone to heaven to be a star but she will always watch over you. He didn't cry. I guess that came later. He just slid off the swing and took my hand and in his childish way said he would look after me instead. And he always has,' Alastair admitted gruffly.

Jenna swallowed hard and slid of the swing and went to him. 'Why are you telling me this, Alastair?' she asked in a small voice.

If it was to make her feel bad for what he thought she had done to Ross's heart he couldn't make her feel any worse. But then she reasoned that Alastair probably didn't know what was going on in his son's heart. Ross wasn't good at opening up his emotions.

'No reason in particular.' He shrugged under his warm jacket. 'I saw you down here and it's where Ross always used to come when he needed time out. I guess you're needing time out too.'

She nodded and linked her arm through his as they started to stroll back to the Hall. 'I've kept out of everyone's way today,' she admitted. 'I'm not ready to face anyone yet.'

'It's understandable, Jenna. You're forgiven.' He sighed. 'Awful business for your mother and such a dreadful shock to you.'

'Have you always known?'

'Heavens, no. I only found out last night. After you had crashed off to bed I came down and found Yvonne and Ross in a bit of a state. Ross told me about your affair and then left your mother to fill in the rest.' He shook his head. 'I wish she'd been honest with me from the start. There is no shame in what happened to her and she was wrong to think I would have been unsympathetic. But life happens.' He sighed again. 'It's a strange world, Jenna, one that never ceases to amaze me with each passing day. By a quirk of coincidence you planned to marry the one man who has changed all our destinies.'

Jenna frowned. 'How do you mean?'

'If you had picked any other man in Paris to marry your mother wouldn't have reacted the way she did and called for Ross in desperation to reason with you.'

Jenna shivered fearfully at the thought. Yes, any other man but Marcel and she would probably be married by now.

'I never thought of that,' she murmured. 'All the same, it happened.'

'Yes, and it's been an emotional disaster for us all but you mustn't allow it to ruin the rest of your life, Jenna. It will prove that the DeLucs mean more to you than us Camerons.'

'They mean nothing to me, Alastair. I've dealt with that in my mind. How can I think of Gerard as my father when he's a stranger? As for Marcel,' she sighed, 'apart from his talent as an artist I don't think I would have liked him as a brother anyway. Ross won't tell you this but I will. He was engaged to me and had another woman on the side. I only found out when I was in London with Ross.' She smiled ruefully. 'I wondered why he wasn't interested in kissing me let alone making love to me. I didn't realise he was involved with Moyra.'

Alastair laughed. 'It was in the genes then. You've had a lucky escape in more ways than one.' He patted her arm. 'It's done with, Jenna; put it behind you. You'll have to talk it over with your mother of course, but you love each other and it will resolve itself. As for Ross... he said it's all over between you and you are leaving.'

Jenna's heart sunk. So he had confided in his father and told him the same thing he had told her. It was finally over.

'But I don't believe it for a minute,' Alastair went on. 'Ross doesn't give up that easily. He's ferocious in business.'

'But I'm not business, ' Jenna murmured to herself.

Perhaps if she was she might stand a chance. Ross had given up on her and that was different. She had pushed him too far. But she hadn't started out with that intention. Her head had been so stuffed with turmoil, she could scarcely think straight at all and then it had got worse. In defence of her feelings she had accused him of everything she knew deep in her heart not to be true. Absurd to believe he would marry her for anything other than love. But the finality of their last row had truly scared her. He was convinced that she didn't love him.

Well, her head was clear now. She would apologise from deep in her heart and...and hope he would forgive her.

'Where is Ross?' Jenna asked when they reached the Hall.

'He said he was going riding. He'll be back shortly; the night is drawing in. Your mother is in the study, making some phone calls and writing some letters; winding a few things up in Paris to keep her mind off other things. If you feel up to talking to her I think the time would be right for you both.'

Jenna nodded. 'I will.' She smiled suddenly. 'I'll keep her busy while you sneak back upstairs.'

'Good girl,' Alastair chuckled as he tiptoed across the hall.

Jenna would rather have seen Ross first. The more time passed the worse her guilt for punishing him so. Her heart ached to put it right with him, her body ached with longing for him. She wanted to hold him forever and prove her love, over and over.

Taking a deep breath she stepped into the study to face her mother. She closed the door softly behind her.

chapter sixteen

It was but an hour since Ross had dismissed Jenna from his life. No one else was up, so in the solitude of the study Ross routinely went through a list of business calls that needed to be made. He dealt with faxes and e-mails robotically. The drawn-out slog of a take-over, sometimes taking months of intricate negotiations, had never drained him like this.

Since Paris he had never known such anguish in his life. Joy and happiness too but when it all came down to it, more anguish than anything else.

There was little adrenaline left to carry him much further. His cold dismissal of Jenna earlier had been a strategy to jolt her out of her self pity, but what if it didn't work?

He understood every emotion she was going through and sympathised deeply, but surely she must realise that amongst the morass of emotions, all those terrible revelations she had heard, his love for her was rock solid?

It would take time, he reasoned to himself. She had a lifetime of insecurity to deal with in one short night and it was too much to expect from her. It crushed him to think she wanted to battle it on her own and not share it with him, but he understood.

'You remind me of your father,' Yvonne said as she placed a cup of coffee on the desk next to him. 'If you're not careful Jenna will do the same to you as I did to him: walk out on you for lack of attention. She's upstairs, too distraught to open her door and you are down here carrying on as if nothing has happened.'

'I'm not insensitive to Jenna's needs, Yvonne,' he said calmly, refusing to rise to her tirade. 'I tried to reason with her this morning but you can't deliver a blow like last nights and expect her to nonchalantly shrug her shoulders and get on with her life. She's angry and upset and doesn't want to speak to anyone'

Yvonne leaned back against his desk and sighed deeply. 'I'm sorry, Ross. I'm the insensitive one. I know what she must be going through, you too. Your father was wonderful about it all. I should have had no fears where he was concerned, but when you bottle everything up for so long you end up making it far worse than it originally was.'

Ross leaned forward and took her hand. 'I understand and I'm sure Jenna will come round, but it will take time.'

Yvonne looked pained. 'Yes, I'm sure you're right, but she hated us both last night, Ross. Can you ever convince her that your heart was in the right place over this?'

Ross shrugged. There was no answer to that. 'It's in the lap of the gods,' he uttered.

A minute after Yvonne went out of the door, his father came in. Ross steeled himself.

'Awful business, Ross. Yvonne told me all about it. Thank you for making it easier for her.'

He sat himself down on a chair next to the desk and Ross braced himself for another heart to heart. Much as he loved his father he really didn't want to share his heart with anyone else but Jenna at the moment.

'According to Yvonne Jenna believes you only wanted to marry her to save her from Marcel. That's not the message I got when you told us about your affair last night.'

Ross rubbed his forehead. 'It's complicated, Father. Jenna feels betrayed so that's the way she sees it. I'm having one helluva job trying to convince her otherwise.'

Alastair smiled. 'I can imagine. She always did take everything the wrong way. But then it's up to you to put her mind at rest, and you'll win through just as Yvonne and I have done.'

Ross leaned back in his seat and twirled a pen between his fingers. 'Jenna says it's over and she wants to leave.'

'Don't let her, Ross,' Alastair advised worriedly. 'Learn from my mistakes. I let Yvonne go three years ago and it took a heart attack to bring her back.'

Ross smiled thinly. 'I'm not waiting around for a heart attack, father. I told her to go.'

Alastair frowned. 'You're giving up on her? Just as I did with her mother?'

'Jenna isn't Yvonne. Don't take this the wrong way, father, but Jenna is far more resilient than her mother. She's stronger. She'll fight back if I push her hard enough.'

'I don't get this. You're not making sense.'

Ross leaned forward. 'Cast your mind back to some of our business strategies, Father. However hungry we were for a deal we always stayed cool. I remember once, the Rimmer Corporation take-over, six months on and nothing was moving. At the final negotiation meeting, you stood up, folded the paperwork away and said, in no uncertain terms, they could all go to hell. You walked out. Twenty-fours hours later the deal was on your desk.'

'And you are using those tactics on Jenna; calling her bluff?' Alastair said with alarm. 'Where's your damned heart, Ross?'

'Not in my boots anymore where she is concerned,' Ross admitted. 'She's breaking my heart in fact. Business is my talent, father, but I'm pretty hopeless with women, as they keep telling me. I'm trying a business strategy with Jenna, as a second to last resort.'

'You are taking some risk, Ross,' Alastair grimaced. Suddenly he frowned. 'Second to last resort? What's the last one then if that fails?'

Pulling out a desk drawer Ross took a small leather-bound box and flicked the lid for his father. 'An engagement ring for Jenna,' he told him. 'I bought it in London but the moment never seemed right to give it to her.'

Alastair stood up laughing. 'Take my advice, son. Use that as your first and only strategy to win her back. The other is too risky. Telling Jenna the opposite of what you want her to do might back-fire on you this time. A diamond the size of a brick will always win a woman's heart. Stick to the traditional ways, Ross. They never fail.'

Ross smiled to himself as his father shut the door behind him. Huh, words of wisdom from his father who hadn't thought to win his wife back with a diamond the size of a brick. It had taken a heart attack to do that. Besides, he didn't know Jenna as Ross did. A ring wouldn't change her mind. It had to come from within. Calling her bluff must have given her food for thought. He hadn't told her to leave because he *didn't* love her, he'd said it was because he *did*. She could be in no doubt as to how he felt about her and he had no doubt about how she felt for him, but the problem was getting her to cross that boundary of her feelings of hurt and betrayal.

Ross pulled forward some paperwork and stared down at it blindly. He had to be patient. If he wasn't he could blow it.

'How can you think of going out at a time like this?' Alastair reprimanded in the kitchen as Ross strode in later that afternoon.

Ross took the stable keys from behind the door. 'Quite easily Father,' Ross told him tightly. He'd waited all day for some sign of her. Every passing hour grinding him down further. He was beginning to seriously doubt that he was doing the right thing by leaving her to come to her senses. He needed air now because the atmosphere in the Hall was suffocating him.

'All day that poor girl has stayed locked in her room,' Alastair said worriedly. 'Yvonne has tried to talk to her through the door and I feel absolutely powerless to do anything about anything!'

Ross turned to his father before going out the door. 'Father, I don't want you getting into a state over this. Everything is going to be all right. Jenna will come out when she is ready and not before.'

'And if she doesn't?'

Ross smiled. 'I'll talk to her when I get back from my ride,' he said in resignation. 'I guess one of us has to back down over this.'

Alastair looked relieved. 'I knew you'd see sense.'

And what sense was that? Ross wondered as he headed for the stables. It seemed he had no sense where Jenna was concerned. The rest of his life was orderly and secure but with Jenna he just couldn't get it right.

After an hour in the saddle astride Drake, Ross wondered how Jenna had coped with the powerful stallion. He remembered his panic that day on finding out she had gone riding and Charlotte saying she had been asking about Drake the night before. Terror at the thought of anything happening to her had made his head spin and before he could tear after her she had breezed into the kitchen as if she'd been for a canter on a seaside donkey.

Deep inside Jenna was tough and yet adorably vulnerable in other areas. Stubborn too...like Drake.

'Steady, boy,' he tried to soothe the stallion, digging in his heels as Drake suddenly veered away from the hedgerow. A vixen shot out into their path followed by two small cubs. The vixen screamed in alarm, a mother protecting her young, and Drake reared in fright.

Ross struggled for control as Drake went crazy, bucking and rearing his head wildly. The power of the stallion outweighed Ross's strength. Kicking his boots out of the stirrups he prepared himself for the inevitable at the same time trying to pull Drake back from the Lockley Woods where he was wildly heading.

Ross saw the low branch of an oak coming towards

him and could do nothing. He had one last thought as it thudded into his chest, choking the breath from him and flinging him heavily down to the ground. Let me live for Jenna.

'Ross! Ross!' Jenna screamed as she crashed through the dark undergrowth. Waving a powerful flashlight in front of her she sobbed his name over and over.

It was her worst nightmare. Finding Drake grazing in the field beyond the paddock, the saddle hanging askew, his reigns dragging the ground, had terrified her. Not finding Ross was worse.

It had been dark by the time she had finished talking with her mother in the study. They had cried a lot and made their peace with each other. Jenna had emerged emotionally drained but her head was clear at last. She had wanted Ross then. To hold him and to say all that was in her heart. She would never leave him. She wanted to start afresh, to put the past down and to start living their lives together. But he hadn't come back from his ride.

She hadn't approached Alastair for fear of worrying him but had shrugged into boots and a fleece jacket and gone down to the stables to find him, only to discover Drake's stable empty and the other horses restless as if they sensed something was wrong.

Jenna had gone crazy.

'Ross! Ross! she cried, fearing the worst which would be all her fault. She had driven him to this by locking herself away all day. He must have ridden Drake too hard and...

'Jenna!'

She screamed with relief, stumbling on and shining the torch this way and that. She saw him then, sitting against the base of an old oak tree and she flew to him.

'Ouch!' he moaned as she dropped to her knees and threw her arms around him, sobbing with relief.

'Oh, Ross, my love. I found Drake and then I couldn't find you,' she cried in a rush of words. 'Are you hurt? It's all my fault. I love you so much. I thought I would never find you and...'

'Darling, I'm OK,' he reassured her, as he clung to her. 'Drake spooked and threw me. I'm just winded and I must have blacked out. I gave my head a crack when I went down.'

Tears streaming down her cheeks with relief Jenna propped the flashlight against a root so she could look at him properly.

'Oh, my God, your forehead is bleeding!' She plunged a trembling hand into her pocket for her mobile. 'I'll call an ambulance and...'

'Jenna,' Ross laughed softly as he took the phone from her and slipped it into his own pocket. 'I'm fine. I really am.'

He scrambled to his feet, brushing himself down, while Jenna got up, her eyes wide and fearful as she watched him.

'You're *not* all right,' she cried. 'You're swaying!'

Ross reached for her and pulled her into his arms. 'No, my darling, you are,' he laughed as he rained small kisses over her face.

'Oh. Ross,' Jenna moaned as she clung to him fiercely. 'I was sick with worry. Don't ever scare me like that again.'

She kissed him deeply, savouring the woody scent of him, adoring him so much, holding him so tightly.

'How did you know I was riding?' he said at last, brushing strands of damp hair from her face to look into her smoky eyes.

'I was down by the swing and your father found me,' she told him breathlessly. 'We had a talk, Ross, and...' she smiled suddenly. 'He was just, so caring, like you. I asked where you were and he said riding. While I waited for you to come back I spoke with my mother and we've talked things through and then you...you didn't come back.'

'And you came to find me.'

Jenna nodded. 'Forgive me, Ross,' she pleaded in a small voice.

'For coming to find me?' He scooped up the flashlight and with his other arm he held her hard against him as they started back home.

Jenna laughed and wrapped an arm around him. 'No, silly, forgive me for all I accused you of. I was upset Ross and I say mad things sometimes.' She sighed. 'It was all such a shock I couldn't get my head around it, and I needed time.'

'Ross, ' she turned her face up to his and said softly. 'You are all that matters to me. I've always known that but so much else got in the way. I want nothing more than to be wed to you and to start our own family. And there will be no such stress for our children because we aren't a bit like our parents.'

Ross stopped and turned her into his arms; his whole body trembling with emotion against hers. Jenna clung to him and felt his love and his passion for her.

'You're right, my darling,' he breathed into her damp hair. 'I've only ever loved you and wanted you. All those years apart but you were always in my heart. One love, one wife. There will never be another.' He lifted her chin and looked deeply into her eyes. 'Take me home, Jenna.'

He nodded beyond her and Jenna turned her head. They were within sight of the Hall. It was ablaze with lights from every window. It looked like the fairy tale castle she used to imagine when she was small.

Slowly they headed towards it and Jenna murmured with a smile. 'That old mausoleum you call home has delivered at last, Ross.'

'Yes. You drove me out once but you managed to drag me back in the end,' he laughed.

'Our children are going to grow up here, with a doting grandfather and a doting grandmother,' Jenna laughed and then stopped and turned to him.

'Did you hurt yourself when you fell off Drake?' she asked pensively. 'I mean really hurt yourself.'

Ross frowned. 'I might have a few bruises to show for it but no bones broken why?'

Jenna grinned wickedly. 'I want you all to myself for a while.' She took his hand and dragged him towards the Hall. 'We'll take the back stairs because if they catch us it will be champagne and toasts to the future and all that. And Mamma really will want to throw herself into wedding arrangements this time.'

'Hold on,' Ross said, 'take this flashlight a minute and sit down,' he laughed.

Dazed Jenna took the light and realised they had reached the old swing. She sat on the bent wood and linked her arms around the rope and watched as Ross fumbled in his pocket.

He came and stood behind her, leaned over her shoulder and lifted her left hand.

'Marry me, Jenna,' he said softly, as he slipped the sparkling ring on to her finger.

'Oh, Ross,' Jenna breathed emotionally and leapt from the swing to throw her arms around his neck, laughing and crying at the same time. 'It was here it all began. You so mad with me and me so wild. But it won't end here, Ross.' She held his face and kissed his lips. 'We'll bring the children here and tell them how it all began and...'

'And we'll do nothing of the sort,' Ross laughed, tugging at her hand. 'Some secrets are best kept. Now is there anything you need to tell me? You keep mentioning children and ...'

Jenna squeezed his hand tightly. 'I'm just eager to start on our first baby Ross.'

And Ross evidently felt the same way as he took her in his arms in his bedroom and loved her so deeply and passionately and completely that she wondered if her wedding ought to be sooner rather than later. She wanted to fit into her white lacy wedding dress. The one she had dreamed of all her life.

Forthcoming titles from HEARTLINE:

OPPOSITES ATTRACT by Kay Gregory
Although *he* doesn't realise it, Venetia Quinn has been in love with her boss, Caleb, ever since he hired her. To Caleb, she's just one of the boys...but a passion filled night has consequences which neither of them could have anticipated...

DECEPTION by June Ann Monks
As a result of his childhood, Ben has always taken a serious approach to life, so 'Kathy Lam's' arrival – she faints in his arms – makes him realise what he's been missing. 'Kathy' has loved Ben all of her life, but what will happen when he discovers that she's been deceiving him?

TROUBLE AT THE TOP by Louise Armstrong
Highly ambitions and fast-moving Nikki has been appointed to close down a once successful business. The one man who stands in her way is gorgeous and sexy Alexander Davidson...definitely a force to be reckoned with!

APPLES FOR THE TEACHER by Steffi Gerrard
Ellie is an experienced teacher of adults, but finds it incredibly difficult to cope with Chris Martin – the most extraordinary handsome and sexy man she's ever met. In fact, it isn't long before Ellie is beginning to wonder if Chris Martin is all that he seems.

Why not start a new romance today with Heartline Books. We will send you an exciting Heartline romance ABSOLUTELY FREE. You can then discover the benefits of our home delivery service: Heartline Books Direct.

Each month, before they reach the shops, you will receive four brand new titles, delivered directly to your door.

All you need to do, is to fill in your details opposite – and return them to us at the Freepost address.

Please send me my free book:

Name (IN BLOCK CAPITALS)

_____

Address (IN BLOCK CAPITALS)

_____

_____

_____

_____ Postcode _____

Address:
HEARTLINE BOOKS
FREEPOST LON 16243,
Swindon SN2 8LA

We may use this information to send you offers from ourselves or selected companies, which may be of interest to you.

If you do not wish to receive further offers
from Heartline Books, please tick this box ☐

If you do not wish to receive further offers
from other companies, please tick this box ☐

Once you receive your free book, unless we hear from you otherwise, within fourteen days, we will be sending you four exciting new romantic novels at a price of £3.99 each, plus £1 p&p. Thereafter, each time you buy our books, we will send you a further pack of four titles.

You can cancel at any time! You have no obligation to ever buy a single book.

Heartline Books – romance at its best!

What do you think of this month's selection?

As we are determined to continue to offer you books which are up to the high standard we know you expect from Heartline, we need you to tell us about *your* reading likes and dislikes. So can we please ask you to spare a few moments to fill in the questionnaire on the following pages and send it back to us? And don't be shy – if you wish to send in a form for each title you have read this month, we'll be delighted to hear from you!

Questionnaire

Please tick the boxes to indicate your answers:

1 Did you enjoy reading this Heartline book?

   Title of book: _____

   A lot ☐
   A little ☐
   Not at all ☐

2 What did you particularly like about this book?

   Believable characters ☐
   Easy to read ☐
   Enjoyable locations ☐
   Interesting story ☐
   Good value for money ☐
   Favourite author ☐
   Modern setting ☐

3 If you didn't like this book, can you please tell us why?

   _____

   _____

4 Would you buy more Heartline Books each month if they were available?

Yes ☐
No – four is enough ☐

5 What other kinds of books do you enjoy reading?

Historical fiction ☐
Puzzle books ☐
Crime/Detective fiction ☐
Non-fiction ☐
Cookery books ☐

Other _____

_____

6 Which magazines and/or newspapers do you read regularly?

a) _____

b) _____

c) _____

d) _____

And now a bit about you:

Name _____

Address _____

_____

_____ Postcode _____

Thank you so much for completing this questionnaire.
Now just tear it out and send it in an envelope to:

HEARTLINE BOOKS
PO Box 400
Swindon SN2 6EJ

(and if you don't want to spoil this book, please feel free
to write to us at the above address with your comments
and opinions.)

Code: MI

Have you missed any of the following books:

The Windrush Affairs *by Maxine Barry*

Soul Whispers *by Julia Wild*

Beguiled *by Kay Gregory*

Red Hot Lover *by Lucy Merritt*

Stay Very Close *by Angela Drake*

Jack of Hearts *by Emma Carter*

Destiny's Echo *by Julie Garrett*

The Truth Game *by Margaret Callaghan*

His Brother's Keeper *by Kathryn Bellamy*

Never Say Goodbye *by Clare Tyler*

Fire Storm *by Patricia Wilson*

Altered Images *by Maxine Barry*

Second Time Around *by June Ann Monks*

Running for Cover *by Harriet Wilson*

Yesterday's Man *by Natalie Fox*

Moth to the Flame *by Maxine Barry*

Dark Obsession *by Lisa Andrews*

Once Bitten...Twice Shy *by Sue Dukes*

Shadows of the Past *by Elizabeth Forsyth*

Perfect Partners *by Emma Carter*

Melting the Iceman *by Maxine Barry*

Marrying A Stranger *by Sophie Jaye*

Secrets *by Julia Wild*

Special Delivery *by June Ann Monks*

Bittersweet Memories *by Carole Somerville*

Hidden Dreams *by Jean Drew*

The Peacock House *by Clare Tyler*
Crescendo *by Patricia Wilson*
The Wrong Bride *by Susanna Carr*
Forbidden *by Megan Paul*
Playing with Fire *by Kathryn Bellamy*
Collision Course *by Joyce Halliday*
Illusions *by Julia Wild*
It Had To Be You *by Lucy Merritt*
Summer Magic *by Ann Bruce*
Imposters In Paradise *by Maxine Barry*

Complete your collection by ringing the Heartline Hotline on 0845 6000504, visiting our website <u>www.heartlinebooks.com</u> or writing to us at Heartline Books, PO Box 400, Swindon SN2 6EJ